'You need a *what*?'

The room rocked alarmingly around Pandora as she stared at Ran Masterson in disbelief.

'I need a wife,' he repeated impatiently.

'But...you—you can't mean you really want to marry me?' she stammered.

'I said I needed a wife,' Ran said irritably. 'I didn't say I wanted to marry anyone—least of all you! I need you to pretend to be my wife for a night, that's all.'

Jessica Hart had a haphazard career before she began writing to finance a degree in history. Her experience ranged from waitress, theatre production assistant and outback cook to newsdesk secretary, expedition PA and English teacher, and she has worked in countries as different as France and Indonesia, Australia and Cameroon. She now lives in the north of England, where her hobbies are limited to eating and drinking and travelling when she can, preferably to places where she'll find good food or desert or tropical rain.

Recent titles by the same author:

WORKING GIRL

PART-TIME WIFE

BY

JESSICA HART

MILLS & BOON

All the characters in this book have no existence outside the imagination of the author, and have no relation whatsoever to anyone bearing the same name or names. They are not even distantly inspired by any individual known or unknown to the author, and all the incidents are pure invention.

MILLS & BOON and the Rose Device
are trademarks of the publisher.
Harlequin Mills & Boon Limited,
Eton House, 18–24 Paradise Road, Richmond, Surrey TW9 1SR

© Jessica Hart 1996

ISBN 0 263 79793 7

Set in 10 on 11½ pt Linotron Times
02-9609-56702

Typeset in Great Britain by CentraCet, Cambridge
Made and printed in Great Britain

CHAPTER ONE

'You need a *what*?'

The room rocked alarmingly around Pandora as she stared at Ran Masterson in disbelief. For one wild, extraordinary moment there she could have sworn that he had said that he needed a wife.

'I need a wife,' he repeated impatiently.

Pandora eyed him warily. He didn't *look* as if he was joking. He was standing by the table, hands thrust into his trouser pockets, looking lean and dark and exasperated. Pandora had never seen Ran Masterson look anything *but* exasperated so it was hard to tell whether it was a habitual expression or whether it was just her, but she had a nasty feeling it was the latter. There were intriguing laughter-lines at the edges of his eyes which suggested that he looked quite different when he smiled. Unfortunately, however, smiling had been the last thing on his mind the last time she had seen him. Murderous rage would be a better way to describe his expression then.

So why was he standing in her studio now asking her to marry him?

It had to be a joke. Pandora smiled a little uncertainly as she wiped her hands on a rag. She didn't want to irritate him any further by failing to appreciate his humour, but it was too late to burst into spontaneous laughter. 'You're not serious?'

Ran scowled. 'I'm not in the mood for jokes,' he snapped.

'But...you—can't mean you really want to marry

me?' she stammered, and an appalled expression swept across his face.

'Marry *you*? That's hardly likely, is it?'

Pandora had the unpleasant feeling that she was trapped in some bizarre dream. She had been standing barefoot at the bench, mindlessly dipping bowls into slip, swirling the liquid clay around the insides before throwing out the excess, and trying desperately to think of some way of conjuring up thousands of pounds out of the air, when Ran had suddenly marched into the studio and told her that the only way she could repay that terrible debt was by becoming his wife. Now she was beginning to wonder whether the strain of the last few days had caught up with her. Had she fallen asleep, or was she simply imagining things?

She could feel the slip drying on the back of her hand, and she brushed it off. If this was a dream, it was an extraordinarily convincing one. She shook her head cautiously. 'But I thought you said. . .?'

'I said I needed a wife,' Ran said irritably. 'I didn't say I wanted to marry anyone—least of all you!'

Pandora gave up. 'I'm sorry, but I haven't the faintest idea what you're talking about,' she confessed. 'One minute you say you want me to marry you and the next you don't!'

'Look, it's simple,' said Ran, obviously exasperated by her obtuseness. 'I need you to pretend to be my wife for a night, that's all.'

'Oh, is that all?' Pandora didn't bother to conceal her sarcasm. 'How silly of me not to have guessed straight away!' Throwing the rag onto the workbench, she pulled out a chair and plonked herself down on it with a glare at Ran's irritably prowling figure. 'Is it too much to ask you to explain *why*, or is that supposed to be blindingly obvious as well?'

Ran stopped pacing abruptly, as if surprised by this unexpectedly astringent attack. His dark brows snapped even closer together and Pandora quailed, remembering a little too late that owing a man thirty thousand pounds put you in a poor position to start being sarcastic to him. For a tense moment he glowered across the room at her, then, to her immense relief, he blew out an exasperated breath and yanked out a chair opposite her.

'All right.' His voice was clipped with impatience as he sat down and linked his fingers on the table, frowning down at them as he ordered his thoughts. Pandora watched him nervously. The only, disastrous time she had met him before, everything had gone so horribly wrong that all she had retained was an impression of cool, controlled power, glacial grey eyes and a formidable temper. Now she looked at him, seeing him as if for the first time again.

The girl behind the counter in the local post office had told Pandora that he had been working in Africa for years, and the effects of sun showed in the tanned, weathered skin and the creases around his eyes. He had dark brown hair and the guarded sort of face that seemed ordinary until you noticed the decisive set of his jaw and the intriguing curve of his mouth.

'You know I've inherited Kendrick Hall from my uncle?' Ran glanced up without warning to find her staring at him. His eyes were a cool, watchful grey, and Pandora flushed beneath their uncomfortably penetrating gaze.

Looking away, she nodded. 'I've heard that you want to sell it,' she said—another piece of information she had gleaned about her disagreeable new neighbour in the post office.

Ran gave a brief, humourless laugh. 'If only I could!

Unfortunately, the estate is entailed, and as my uncle's nearest male relative that means I'm not allowed to sell it without going to a lot of legal expense to break the entail.'

'Why don't you just live in it?' asked Pandora, thinking that most people would be glad to own a beautiful old house in the unspoilt Northumbrian countryside. 'It's a lovely area.'

'It may be lovely but it's not exactly convenient when you work in East Africa,' said Ran with some asperity.

'Couldn't you work here?' She wasn't quite sure why they were discussing Ran's job at a time like this, but at least it was better than talking about the money she owed him or the bizarre proposal he had made.

'No, I couldn't,' said Ran coldly. 'I'm a consultant in land management to the Mandibian government with a special brief to set up a whole new department to deal with some of the agricultural problems there. Mandibia has the potential to be a great country, and they're investing a lot of money and hopes in the new department. I've got a couple of months' leave to sort out things here, but frankly I'd rather be out in the field getting on with the job than messing around trying to look after a great big house I don't even want.'

He paused and frowned across at Pandora, who was thinking how easily she could imagine a country entrusting its future to a man like Ran Masterson. There was a quality of tough, dynamic competence about him that was both unsettling and reassuring. He was the kind of man you wanted on your side, the kind of man who could solve any problem. A man used to getting his own way, a man unprepared to suffer fools gladly. *Not* the kind of man you wanted to antagonise by breaking one of his priceless family heirlooms.

The thought recalled Pandora to the present with a

shudder. She still didn't understand why she was supposed to repay that awful debt by pretending to be Ran's wife. Her eyes rested unthinkingly on his cool, firm mouth and an odd feeling snaked down her spine. The whole idea was preposterous, of course. Preposterous and dangerous and disturbing and alarmingly, inexplicably easy to visualise.

'What's all this got to do with me?' she asked on a half-gasp.

'I'm coming to that,' said Ran sharply. 'Given that I've got an important job to do in Africa, and that I can't just sell Kendrick Hall, I've decided my best bet is to turn it into an exclusive guest house. I'm told that foreign tourists are prepared to pay a good deal for the privilege of staying in a country house as if they were private guests, and it's easier and less expensive than trying to set up a hotel. Someone put me in touch with an American agency which arranges visits for their clients, and the directors came to look round briefly this morning.' He stopped, as if reluctant to continue.

'And?' said Pandora, still unsure where all this was leading.

'And they liked it very much,' Ran said slowly. 'The house needs considerable renovation, of course, but once it's been modernised and redecorated they seemed to think it would be very suitable for their clients.' He paused and glanced at Pandora. 'There was only one real problem.'

'What was that?' she asked, with the sinking feeling that she was about to enter the story.

'They thought their clients would prefer it if I had a wife to act as hostess.' Ran appeared to be picking his words with care. 'Once the house is restored, I'm planning to turn it over to a couple who will be able to manage the bookings, cook for the guests and so on.

Unfortunately Myra and Elaine—the two directors—assumed that I would be host myself. Apparently the idea is that their clients feel as if they're guests of the family. I could see they were on the point of turning me down when they found out that I wasn't married, but, having got that far, I was damned if I was going to give up, so I said that there had been some misunderstanding and that I did have a wife; it was just that she wasn't there at the moment.'

Pandora looked at him dubiously. 'That must have sounded a bit odd.'

He shrugged. 'I convinced them that as we'd only just got back from Africa my wife had gone to visit her family. It seemed reasonable enough. Unfortunately I then made the mistake of saying that she would be joining me next week, and what a pity it was that they wouldn't be able to meet her.' Ran sighed in exasperated remembrance. 'At which point Elaine promptly suggested that they stop here again on their way back from Edinburgh. She said it would be such a good opportunity to see Kendrick Hall again and to meet you.'

'To meet *me*?'

There was a slight pause. 'I told them my wife was called Pandora,' he said evenly at last, and looked directly into her eyes.

Pandora's heart did a breathless somersault into her throat. 'What on earth made you give them my name?' she asked in a rather high voice.

For the first time, Ran looked uncertain. 'You just came to mind,' he said, and his eyes narrowed as he stared at her as if trying to recall the vision that had come to him of a coltishly slender girl with a heart-shaped face, wide violet-blue eyes and a cloud of soft, dark hair. An odd expression flickered briefly in his eyes, to be replaced by exasperated disapproval as he registered the reality sitting opposite him now. There was a smear of clay on Pandora's cheek, her hair had been ineffectively tied back and was falling over her face and her old beige cardigan had holes at each elbow.

'I can't imagine why I thought of *you*,' he went on, looking down his nose. 'You're the last person I would associate with the idea of a wife, but I had to think of a name on the spur of the moment and yours was the best I could come up with.'

'Charming!' muttered Pandora, obscurely offended. It wasn't that she wanted him to like her particularly, but if he wanted her to act as his wife he could have been a little less disparaging.

'Anyway,' Ran continued briskly, 'once I'd had a chance to think about it, it didn't seem quite such a stupid idea. I've only been here for a week so I don't know anyone in this part of the country, and the only other girl I could ask is in the States at the moment. At least you've got the advantage of being a stranger here too—or have you already acquired some boyfriend to make things awkward?' His tone made it clear that he didn't think it likely that any man could be interested in a scruffy potter with a holey cardigan.

Pandora wrapped the offending cardigan around her in an unconsciously defensive gesture. She was very fond of it. 'I haven't had time to meet anyone yet,' she said, wishing she could admit to a string of palpitating lovers to match that girl in the States he had mentioned so casually.

'Well, then,' he said as if that settled the matter, and glanced at his watch. 'It may be a bit harder for you to act like a normal wife, but it'll only be for twenty-four hours so even you should be able to manage that.'

'Can't you ask someone else?' grumbled Pandora, still huffy. 'I'm really busy at the moment.' She waved an arm at the trays of pottery waiting to be fired. 'I've got an exhibition coming up in less than three weeks.' She couldn't quite keep the note of pride from her voice. It wouldn't do Ran Masterson any harm to know that she was good enough to have her own exhibition.

Ran was unimpressed. 'I'm not asking you to pretend to be my wife, Pandora,' he said in a dangerously quiet voice. 'I'm telling you.'

'You can't do that!' she protested, making as if to stand up, but he reached coolly across the table and grasped her wrist with a hard hand. His fingers were strong and warm against her skin and although he didn't exert any force Pandora found herself sinking back down into her chair. He took away his hand and she stared down at where he had held her. Her wrist was tingling, stinging, as if his touch was scorched into her skin.

'And you can't produce the thirty thousand pounds you owe me, can you?' he said softly. 'Or had you forgotten that particular little incident?'

If only she could!

It had been her own fault for not keeping Homer on the lead. Celia had told her not to let him into the Kendrick Hall gardens, but they had been almost back at the stables and Pandora had been exhausted after being towed along the empty lanes. The entrance to the old stable block had been in sight when she'd bent and slipped off the lead, expecting that the dog would rush ahead to wait for a biscuit at the front door. Instead, he'd given an excited yelp, dropped his nose to his paws and, with a naughty, flickering look, belted off down the avenue towards Kendrick Hall.

Not for the first time, Pandora had wished that her

godmother had a preference for timid chihuahuas instead of for huge, reprobate mongrels that were the despair of the animal-rescue services. She'd called to him but when, as expected, he'd taken absolutely no notice, she'd trudged resignedly after him without the slightest suspicion that her life was about to change completely. At that stage Pandora had been unduly concerned. It wasn't as if there had been anyone around for Homer to annoy. Kendrick Hall had lain empty since old Eustace Masterson had died and, although rumour in the post office had had it that the house had been inherited by a nephew, there had been no sign of him yet.

It hadn't been until she'd seen the open front door that her confidence had faltered, and when the sound of barking had come from inside the house she'd begun to run. 'Homer! Come here at once!'

She skidded to a halt in the doorway. It opened into a huge hall, crammed with such an extraordinary collection of artefacts that for a moment Pandora forgot to feel relieved that there was no one else there to witness Homer's disgrace and simply stood and gaped. The soaring stone walls were hung with an assortment of dusty antlers, stuffed fish, a sad collection of heads including a lugubrious water buffalo, and a mind-boggling array of weaponry. A vast, grimy chandelier hung from the ceiling, and the floor was cluttered with heavy wooden furniture, interspersed with the odd suit of armour, an exquisite Chinese vase and a hideously realistic python coiled convincingly up a log. In the middle of it all stood Homer, barking furiously at an enormous stuffed bear.

Pandora gathered her wits together. 'Homer!' she called sternly, and advanced on him, but he skittered away, nearly colliding with a man who had emerged abruptly from a door on the far side of the hall.

'What the hell is going on?' he demanded furiously.

Pandora had a confused impression of brown, rangy strength and exasperation as she lunged unsuccessfully at Homer. 'I'm so sorry...' she gasped over the sound of barking, and straightened, pushing the cloudy hair away from her face. She found herself facing a tanned, angry-looking man with joltingly hard grey eyes and the kind of lean, tough physique that belonged with wide, empty horizons. He looked as if he should be bowling along a dusty road in a beaten-up Jeep or sitting astride a horse squinting into the sun instead of standing in this bizarrely cluttered old hall.

Pandora swallowed. 'I'm sorry,' she began again, and took an ineffectual step towards Homer, but the man forestalled her. Grasping the dog's collar in one hard hand, he ordered him to sit. To Pandora's astonishment, Homer sat.

'Oh, thank you!' she sighed, and smiled at the stranger in relief.

Pandora had a peculiarly sweet smile, but it had little effect on the man. 'Who are you?' he asked brusquely. 'And what are you doing in my house?'

'*Your* house?' In spite of her embarrassment, Pandora eyed him with new interest. 'Then you must be Eustace Masterson's nephew?'

'I'm Ran Masterson, yes,' he said. His voice was cool and clipped, with an edge of irritated astringency. 'I know who I am. I still don't know who *you* are.'

'My name's Pandora Greenwood.' Pandora thought about offering to shake hands, but Ran Masterson's expression was hardly encouraging, so she decided against it, wrapping her cardigan around her instead.

'We're neighbours. I'm living in the converted stables at the end of the drive.'

If Ran was pleased to discover a new neighbour, he showed absolutely no sign of it. He frowned. 'I thought the solicitor told me the stables were owned by people called Williams?'

'John and Celia.' Pandora nodded. 'Celia's my god-mother. John's got a visiting professorship to a university in Texas and I'm looking after Homer while they're away.' She gestured down at the dog who was looking innocent with Ran's hand firmly on his collar.

'You don't seem to be making a very good job of it,' said Ran blisteringly, and she flushed.

'No, I'm sorry. He ran down here before I could catch him. I don't usually let him off the lead near the house.'

'So I should hope,' he said, with a disapproving look down at the shaggy dog by his side. 'The last thing I need at the moment is a wild dog running all over the grounds.'

'It won't happen again,' Pandora promised in a small voice, and began to edge towards the door.

'Make sure it doesn't.' Ran released Homer's collar. 'Here, you'd better put him on the lead before he does any damage.'

Pandora reached down but before she could catch hold of him Homer had caught sight of the bear looming behind her and erupted into a volley of barks as he darted away.

Ran swore unpleasantly. 'Haven't you got any control over that dog?'

'Homer!' she pleaded, but the dog dodged away and into the delicate stand that held the Chinese vase.

After that, things seemed to happen in slow motion. The stand rocked from side to side before toppling slowly sideways, and the vase began falling in a graceful curve. Pandora watched, horrified, forcing her frozen limbs into action too late to catch it. Arms still outstretched, she landed on her knees just as the fragile porcelain smashed onto the stone floor.

There was a long moment of utter stillness and silence. Pandora closed her eyes. She didn't dare move, didn't dare speak.

'Do you know what you've done?' The words were innocuous enough but the tone was so savage that Pandora winced and opened her eyes. Ran Masterson was crouched beside her, reverently picking up the largest pieces. In spite of his tan, he was white about the mouth and the grey eyes blazed with fury.

'I—I'm. . .' she stammered, and he rounded on her.

'You're what? Sorry?' His voice lashed at her.

She nodded miserably.

'Your dog's just broken a vase worth thirty thousand pounds and you're *sorry*?'

Pandora went white. '*Th-thirty*. . .?'

'Thirty thousand pounds,' Ran confirmed through his teeth. 'I had a dealer round only yesterday. I was going to sell it to pay for the restoration of the house,' he went on in the same terrifyingly tight voice. 'I'm not going to get very much for it now, am I?'

Of course, Pandora offered to pay him back. Ran looked her up and down, noting the faded skirt and the worn cardigan, and asked contemptuously if she had a spare thirty thousand. Pandora felt sick at the very thought of such a huge sum of money. There was no way she could even raise a tenth of it. She barely covered her costs with her pottery and there was no question of approaching her parents. They had struggled as it was to put her through art college.

Ran, summing up her financial situation without

difficulty, announced curtly that he would contact the Williamses directly. Homer was their dog, and they at least had a house to sell. Desperate, Pandora begged him for a week to try and raise the money herself. She owed so much to her godmother. How could she possibly repay her by landing her with a debt like this?

But how could she possibly repay Ran Masterson?

After four days of agonising, Pandora was no nearer to finding a solution. And now, on this wet June afternoon, he was sitting across the table from her honestly expecting her to convince perfect strangers that she was his wife.

'Well?' he said in a hard voice. 'Are you going to repay your debt or am I going to get my solicitor to ring the Williamses?'

Pandora chewed her lower lip. 'Can I just get this straight? If I agree to help convince these Americans that I'm your wife, you'll forget about the vase?'

'That's it.'

'Can you afford to wipe out a debt like that?' she asked him, knowing that it was unwise to look a gift horse in the mouth but unable to prevent her suspicions.

Ran shrugged. 'I didn't know how valuable the vase was until that antiques dealer came round. If I'd been able to sell it, it would have gone a long way towards solving Kendrick Hall's financial problems. The whole house is riddled with damp and needs to be completely renovated. I don't want to use my own income, so the house is going to have to pay for itself somehow. Thanks to you and your dog, I'll have to sell rather more of the pictures than I'd hoped. I don't think one night's pretence is too much to ask in exchange for that, do you? It's not as if I'm asking you to spend the rest of your life with me, after all. A cup of tea, a few drinks, dinner, then we all retire to bed. What's the problem with that?'

'That rather depends on whose bed you're retiring to!'

'So that's what you're worried about!' Ran sat back in his chair and eyed Pandora sardonically. 'Do you really think this is an elaborate ruse to get you into bed, Pandora?'

She flushed at his tone. 'Of course not!'

'That's just as well, because I can assure you that I've got more important things on my mind at the moment than a silly, scruffy, irresponsible girl,' he told her in a stinging voice that deepened the colour in her cheeks even further. 'For all I know you may have a delectable body under all those ethnic layers, but I hardly think it's likely to be worth thirty thousand pounds, and frankly I'm not interested in whether it is or not.

'All I'm interested in is getting this guest house scheme off the ground so that I can get back to doing what I do best in Africa. If that means spending a night with you, that's what I'll do. I'm sure we'd both prefer not to sleep together but Myra and Elaine might wonder if they saw a supposedly happily married couple creeping off to separate bedrooms, and, when it comes down to it, convincing them to send their clients here means more to me than your delicate feelings!'

'All right, all right,' said Pandora crossly, pushing back her chair and getting restlessly to her feet. 'I've got the point. As long as it's clear that my wifely role stops at the bedroom door.'

Ran gave her a saturnine look from his chair. 'So you will do it?'

'I don't have much choice, do I?' she retorted with some bitterness. 'You know perfectly well that I'll never be able to find thirty thousand pounds, and I can't ask John and Celia to pay.'

'Why not?' said Ran. 'It was their dog that broke the vase, after all.'

Pandora rested her hand protectively on Homer's shaggy head. 'Yes, but they left him with me. That was the whole idea. I wanted to see if I could make a real go of the pottery, but I didn't have anywhere to work, so Celia suggested I live here and use her studio while they were away in return for looking after Homer. She was the one who originally got me interested in pottery and she's always been so encouraging. If it wasn't for her, I'd never have got this far. I *couldn't* repay her by landing her with such a huge debt!'

'You should have thought of that before you let that animal off the lead,' said Ran unsympathetically.

'You should have thought of stray dogs before you left your door open and thirty thousand-pound vases precariously balanced above a stone floor,' Pandora was provoked into retorting, and met his glare with a challenging look.

'I'd have thought you would be grateful to be getting off so lightly,' he reminded her ominously, but she only pushed her hair away from her face, her violet eyes bright and defiant.

'If you can call sleeping with a perfect stranger "getting off lightly"!'

Ran stood up abruptly. 'You can pay me the thirty thousand pounds if you prefer,' he said indifferently. 'I should be able to buy a professional actress for that.'

She should have remembered her first impression of a man who always got his own way in the end. Seeing him heading for the door, Pandora realised that her bluff was being called and she put out a hand. 'No!'

Ran turned with his hand on the latch and raised an

enquiring eyebrow. 'All right, I'm sorry,' she said a little sullenly. 'I'll do whatever you want.'

'That's better,' he said crisply, returning. 'I don't know what you're making all this fuss about.'

'It's just such a crazy idea!' said Pandora. She gestured down at her threadbare jeans and plucked at the missing elbows of her cardigan. 'You were the one who said I looked a mess. No one's ever going to believe I'm your wife.'

'They will if you smarten yourself up a bit.' Ran took her by the shoulders so that he could inspect her with a critical eye. 'You're a pretty girl now that I look at you,' he said impersonally, looking her up and down, narrowing his eyes as he studied the smooth warmth of her skin, the dark, silky mass of hair and her almost clumsy slenderness. 'In fact,' he added reflectively as his gaze returned to the clear lines of her face, 'you could be quite beautiful if you took a little trouble with yourself.'

Pandora felt a great wave of heat sweep over her. She was acutely conscious of his eyes on her face, of his hands on her shoulders. They were brown and strong and their touch seemed to vibrate through her, along her collar-bone, down her arm, shivering down her spine, behind her knees, past her ankles to her toes. Swallowing, she stared at his jaw, unable to meet his eyes, afraid to look at his mouth.

Until now he had been a problem, a source of indignation and desperate worry. Now, suddenly, he was a disconcertingly attractive man—a man she was going to have to sleep with in just a few days' time.

'Myra and Elaine won't think there's anything odd about you being my wife if you wear a decent dress for a change.' Oblivious to her perturbation, Ran was continuing in the same impersonal tone. To Pandora's relief, he dropped his hands from her shoulders. 'You must have something smarter to wear than what you've got on at the moment.'

'Not really,' she mumbled, wondering how it was possible to still feel his hands burning through the wool cardigan and the cotton shirt onto her skin when they were back in his trouser pockets. 'I've got a sort of evening dress my mother gave me, but otherwise I only have clothes to work in and there's not much point in being smart when you're working with clay.'

'Obviously not,' said Ran, with a disparaging look down at her clothes. 'Well, in that case we'll just have to buy you something when we go to get the photograph taken.'

Pandora blinked. 'What photograph?'

'Our wedding photograph. A framed studio portrait commemorating our wedding standing around in the drawing room should add a little corroborative detail, don't you think?'

'I suppose so,' she said dubiously, moving away from his suddenly disturbing nearness with studied casualness. He had obviously thought everything through. 'When are we going to get that done?'

'Tomorrow, I hope. I'll ring the photographer this afternoon and pick you up in the morning. We might as well go into Wickworth together and do everything at once.'

'I thought I was only going to be on call for twenty-four hours,' Pandora objected. 'When am I going to fire my pots?'

'You can do that in the afternoon.'

'I really can't afford to spend a whole morning in Wickworth. . .' she began, but Ran held up a hand.

'What was that you said about doing anything I wanted?' he reminded her unpleasantly.

Pandora subsided, grumbling under her breath, 'You'd better tell me what else I'm expected to do while you're at it!'

'You'll have to come to the house so that you know your way around before they arrive,' he told her. 'And since you're going to be there anyway you might as well make yourself useful by preparing their rooms and making the house look as nice as possible—you could clean the silver, arrange some flowers, that sort of thing.'

Pandora sighed. She hated doing housework. 'Anything else?' she asked with a long-suffering look.

'You'll have to produce some meals. They'll be expecting you to be a good cook.'

'But I've got no idea about cooking!'

Ran took a step forward so that he was standing very close and Pandora found herself backed up against the kiln with no room to manoeuvre. 'Then you'll just have to make a big effort, won't you?' he said. 'I'm not writing off a debt like that for nothing, Pandora. You are going to convince those Americans not only that you're my wife, but also that their guests will think you the hostess with the mostest. Is that understood?'

Pandora nodded reluctantly, but he didn't move away. 'That means that you are going to put everything you've got into making the house as welcoming as possible. You're going to cook a delicious dinner. And you're going to behave like a happily married wife, and not like a sullen girl who doesn't appreciate her luck at getting out of paying an enormous debt. If you don't think you can do that, you'd better tell me now and think about finding thirty thousand pounds instead!'

She looked into implacable grey eyes, the eyes of a man who meant exactly what he said, and she swallowed. 'I can do it,' she said.

CHAPTER TWO

IT WAS just a job.

That was what Pandora told herself, anyway. Ran was right. Pretending to be his wife was a small price to pay in recompense for breaking such an heirloom. It was just that whenever she thought about him, about spending the night with him, her stomach began to churn with a turbulent mixture of alarm and nervous excitement.

Of course, it was natural to feel nervous at the prospect of sharing a room with a complete stranger, Pandora reassured herself. She just wished her nervousness weren't so bound up with the memory of how warm his fingers had been around her wrist, how strong his hands had felt on her shoulders. As she lay in bed that night, with Homer snoring noisily on the floor beside her, she rehearsed again and again all the reasons why pretending to be Mrs Ran Masterson was a perfectly straightforward arrangement and absolutely nothing to be worried about, but just when she thought she had convinced herself she remembered those cool eyes and that cool mouth and those warm hands, and suddenly *nothing* was straightforward any more.

All in all, it took Pandora a long time to get to sleep. She was woken the next morning by Homer's cold nose nudging beneath the duvet, and groped blearily for her watch. It was five to nine.

'Oh, God, and he's coming to pick me up at half past nine!' yelped Pandora, shoving Homer aside without bothering to explain who 'he' was. Ran had rung her the previous evening, as cool and clipped as ever, telling her to be dressed and ready at half past nine. 'And perhaps you could make a little more effort with your clothes,' he had added stringently. 'I'm not taking Orphan Annie out to lunch.'

Splashing water frantically on her face, Pandora brushed her teeth as she gloomily surveyed her wardrobe. Apart from that one dress her mother had insisted on giving her, she just didn't *have* anything smart to wear. Still, there wasn't much she could do about it now, she decided, resigned, stepping into a skirt patterned in browns and blacks and greens and pulling on a loose fawn cotton jumper with some difficulty as her toothbrush was still in her mouth. At least neither the skirt nor the jumper had any holes—not obvious ones, anyway.

There was no time for breakfast. Whistling for Homer, Pandora opened the door to a sweet June morning. Yesterday's rain had left the hedgerows lush and green and the sun was trembling on the damp leaves. It was much too nice a day to keep Homer on the lead when he was going to have to spend the whole morning shut up indoors. Pandora let him snuffle ahead while she walked more slowly along the lane, enjoying the feel of the soft air on her face. Kendrick Hall and its stables were isolated in the rolling Northumberland countryside below the Cheviots, and only a few tractors ever came along these roads.

Pandora glanced at her watch. They would have to go back. Ran Masterson didn't strike her as a man who would be particularly tolerant of unpunctuality. She looked round for Homer in time to see him disappearing into a hedge, tail wagging furiously. Heart sinking, Pandora hurried over. Fortunately he had been diverted by a particularly pungent smell, so she was able to catch him, but it meant clambering across a ditch and half burying herself in the hedge before she could grab hold of his collar. A struggle ensued which left Pandora breathless and tousled and covered with half the hedge, but she eventually managed to drag the dog back onto the road.

By this time it was already nine-thirty. Keeping a firm hold of the lead, Pandora began to run. Entering into the spirit of the game, Homer galloped ahead of her, jumping up to lick her face and barking encouragingly. The noise drew Ran out of the stable courtyard to stare at the sight of Pandora being towed down the lane behind the disreputable-looking dog, her cheeks pink with exertion and her hair liberally sprinkled with bits of twig and grass.

'I'm sorry I'm late,' she panted as they came up and Homer proceeded to greet Ran, in spite of all evidence to the contrary, as an old friend.

'Down!' said Ran firmly before the dog could jump all over his suit. Homer dropped his ears placatingly and contented himself with sniffing at Ran's ankles and wagging his tail with pleasure. Ran turned to Pandora and looked her over with disapproving grey eyes. 'Where on earth have you been?'

'I had to take Homer for a walk before I shut him in.' Next to Ran's cool composure, Pandora felt hot and bothered and even more breathless than before. He was looking guarded in an immaculate grey suit with a white shirt and a pale grey tie. The formal clothes should have looked odd with that quality of quiet, rangy strength that was so much part of him, but instead they made him seem tougher and more contained than ever.

'It looked to me as if he was taking *you* for a walk,' said Ran caustically, and brushed a leaf from her shoulder. 'Is there some reason why you're wearing half the countryside?'

He had barely touched her, yet Pandora could feel her shoulder burning with awareness. Such stupid sensitivity made her cross, and she brushed impatiently at her hair and jumper. 'I had to drag Homer out of a hedge,' she said shortly. 'I'll just put him inside and then we can go.'

'Aren't you going to change?'

She looked at him in surprise. 'What do you mean?'

'I thought I told you to wear something smart.'

'This *is* smart!'

Ran frowned irritably. 'You must be able to do better than that! Not even you would expect to get married in something that resembles a rag and a piece of sacking!'

'I didn't expect to be getting married when I came away,' Pandora reminded him with some sarcasm, making her way to the house. 'If I had, then of *course* I would have brought my long white dress and veil which I've had hanging in the wardrobe at home just in case someone pops the question unexpectedly!'

'No one's expecting you to produce a bride's dress,' snapped Ran. 'But you must have something more suitable for a wedding photograph than a brown jumper!'

'Well, I haven't,' said Pandora childishly.

He sighed with exasperation. 'I suppose you'll just have to buy something suitable in Wickworth. I dare say it's not the fashion capital of the north, but you must be able to find something better than what you've got on!'

'I don't see that it matters,' she grumbled, offended, as she shut Homer into the kitchen, having removed anything remotely chewable out of his reach and picked up an apple to eat in the car. 'Why can't the photographer do a head and shoulders shot?'

'Because I've told the photographer that we want a picture to commemorate our wedding and it'll look decidedly odd if I turn up in a suit while you're dressed with the same effort you'd use if you were going to weed the garden!'

Pandora took a defiant bite of her apple as they walked out to his car. She got in and pulled the door to with unnecessary force. 'It all sounds odd anyway,' she said through the mouthful of apple. She was normally quite oblivious to what she was wearing, but Ran's disparaging comments had left her feeling unusually affronted. 'If we wanted a photograph, why wouldn't we have had it taken on our wedding day?'

'We might have got married on the spur of the moment.' Ran was obviously exasperated by Pandora's questioning of the story he had prepared.

'I can't imagining you doing anything that romantic,' said Pandora provocatively.

'I can't imagine doing anything that stupid,' he retorted, shooting her a nasty look as he reversed the car out of the courtyard. 'But the photographer is not to know that the idea of me getting married at all, let alone on the spur of the moment and to someone as disastrously unsuitable as you, is practically inconceivable, is he?'

'Why, what have you got against marriage?' she asked, continuing to munch on the apple and deciding to ignore his unflattering reference to her.

'Everything,' he said shortly. 'Other people can fall over themselves to get married, but I intend to avoid that particular trap.'

Pandora peeked at him sideways from under her lashes, wondering why he was so vehemently anti-marriage. He was glancing in the rear-view mirror, and the line of his jaw and throat was very clear in the bright morning light. Everything about him was suddenly definite—the slight furrow of concentration between his brows, the arrogant line of his nose, the unexpectedly dark lashes fringing the pale eyes. Pandora's gaze slid down to the cool, disturbing mouth and abruptly her stomach disappeared.

She jerked her eyes away. It was easier to think about how grumpy and disagreeable he was than to wonder why looking at his mouth always had that odd effect on her.

'So, the story is that we were so in love we couldn't wait to arrange a traditional wedding?' she said in a determinedly brisk voice.

'Something like that,' said Ran with distaste.

'If we couldn't be bothered with all the fuss then, why are we bothering to get a photograph done now?'

'I don't know,' he said irritably. 'To send to your sick mother in Canada or something.'

'But my mother lives in Dorset!'

'Look, it doesn't matter *where* your mother lives!' Ran's mouth was thin with exasperation. 'It's none of the photographer's business anyway. He just needs to take a picture of us looking as if we might conceivably be in love with one another.'

'Well, let's hope he's creative,' said Pandora with some tartness. 'He's going to have his work cut out making *you* look like a man in love! I've never seen anyone look less lover-like.'

He shot her an unpleasant look. 'How would you like me to look?'

'You could look a little more. . .friendly.'

'Would you look friendly if someone had smashed your priceless family heirloom?'

'Anyone would think I'd thrown it onto the floor deliberately,' grumbled Pandora, jamming her apple core into the ashtray and deliberately ignoring his glower. 'It was Homer who broke the vase, not me, if you remember. I don't know why you didn't insist on Homer acting as your bride. At least you might look more pleased to be with him!'

'Don't be ridiculous!' A muscle was twitching in Ran's jaw. 'We're both going to have to act when we get to the photographer—and it would help if you looked the part. I've got an appointment with the solicitor first, so you can go and buy an outfit while I'm with him.'

Pandora heaved a martyred sigh. She hated buying clothes. 'What sort of outfit did you have in mind?'

'I'm not a fashion expert,' he said unhelpfully.

'You'd never guess from the way you carry on about my clothes,' she muttered under her breath and he glanced at her sharply.

'Just buy something *suitable*. A dress, a suit. . .whatever you'd wear if you were getting married for real.'

Easier said than done, Pandora thought some half an hour later, looking gloomily through the clothes racks in the high-street shops. Wickworth was a fair-sized market town, but it wasn't exactly notable for its stylish shops. Ran had given her a huge wad of twenty-pound notes and told her to meet him at the hotel 'at eleven o'clock *sharp*' complete with a wedding outfit. 'Yes, *sir*!' Pandora had saluted his receding back, reflecting that if he could afford to hand out that much just for a dress he could probably afford another Chinese vase without too much trouble.

She had tried all the chain-stores without success and was getting desperate by the time she braved the intimidatingly expensive-looking boutique behind the market square. It wasn't the kind of shop she would normally have dreamed of entering, but time was ticking on and she didn't dare tell Ran that she hadn't been able to find anything. The sales assistant raised her brows at Pandora's somewhat dishevelled appearance, but Pandora had decided that it was time to seek help.

'I'm getting married tomorrow,' she said ingenuously, 'and I can't find anything to wear!'

The sales assistant brightened. 'What sort of thing were you looking for?'

'My fiancé wants me to look smart,' said Pandora, glad that this was a shop she was never likely to patronise again.

Before she quite knew what was happening, she found herself hustled into a changing room with a number of outfits whose price tags made her blench. The sales assistant had evidently warmed to the challenge of transforming Pandora and bullied her into one outfit after the other to the accompaniment of endless questions about what sort of wedding it was to be, where they would go on their honeymoon, what her fiancé was like.

'He's very. . .forceful,' said Pandora, who was beginning to feel bamboozled by all these questions. Acting convincingly was harder work than she had realised.

'I suppose he's very attractive too?' said the sales assistant, sighing sentimentally.

A vision of Ran rose before Pandora with such clarity that she stopped in the act of wriggling into a dress. She could picture him exactly, she realised: every plane, every line of his face, the compact strength of his body and the warm, sure hands. *Were* those laughter-lines around his eyes? She had never seen him smile. What would a laugh do to those cool eyes and that cool, cool mouth? Something turned over inside Pandora and she straightened abruptly.

'He's all right,' she said.

The other woman looked disappointed, but then she caught sight of Pandora's reflection in the mirror. 'That's perfect on you! Here, try the jacket with it.'

Pandora regarded herself dubiously. She looked completely different in the simply tailored dress with the short matching jacket. The warm, creamy yellow colour flattered her skin and set off her dark mass of hair. 'I don't know that it's really *me*.'

'It looks wonderful,' said the assistant firmly. 'Elegant and sophisticated. All you need now are shoes and a hat.'

Pandora allowed herself to be persuaded into a pair of shoes, but she drew the line at the tasteful hat proffered. She had found a suitable outfit as instructed, but Ran hadn't said anything about a hat, had he? 'I'll take that one,' she said, pointing to the hat in the window which had originally caught her eye. Decorated with an extravagant bow, it had a huge rim which dipped down over one eye. It was so excessive that Ran would be appalled.

It was perfect.

Feeling very pleased with herself, Pandora handed over almost all the money Ran had given her and went off to follow the sales assistant's advice about lipstick. If Ran wanted her transformed, transformed she would be!

Ran was reading a newspaper in one of the comfortable leather armchairs that dotted the foyer of Wickworth's only four-star hotel when Pandora burst through the doors, having belatedly realised that she was ten minutes late. Lowering the paper, he looked at her over the top of it, his grey eyes light and disapproving.

'You're late.'

'Only ten minutes.' It must have been hurrying down the high street that had left her so breathless. It couldn't be anything to do with the feeling that gripped her when she saw him rise to his feet, so cool and restrained and yet somehow so definite. He didn't do anything to draw attention to himself, but there was an indefinable quality about him that made him the focus of the entire room.

He looked at his watch. 'Fourteen minutes,' he corrected her.

'Oh, all right, *fourteen* minutes.' Pandora waved her bags at him. 'Do you want to see what I bought?'

'I'd like to see it on,' said Ran, glancing meaningfully at his watch again. 'We're due at the photographer's at half past.'

Pandora nearly lost her nerve as she changed in the Ladies. 'I'll never be able to carry it off,' she muttered to her unfamiliar reflection as she carefully applied the lipstick she had bought. Her face looked back at her, bright and bold. At least Ran wouldn't be able to complain that she looked exactly the same. The hat really *was* a bit much. . . Pandora smoothed down her jacket a little nervously and decided it might be better to introduce the hat to Ran gradually.

He had gone back to his paper, evidently expecting her to be ages, and he was unaware of Pandora's approach until she was right beside him. 'Well, what do you think?'

Lowering the paper, Ran glanced up, only to freeze as he saw the svelte, sophisticated figure standing by his chair, absurd hat in hand and tilted violet eyes uncertain. For a moment he looked utterly blank, then he blinked and rose slowly to his feet.

'Do I look all right?' asked Pandora doubtfully when he still didn't say anything. Perhaps he thought she looked ridiculous after all?

'Why, yes. . .' Ran seemed to realise that his voice sounded odd and cleared his throat. 'You look. . .fine.'

Fine? Was that all he could say? Up to now, Pandora hadn't even admitted to herself how much she wanted to impress him, to make him see her differently. It would obviously take more than an expensive suit. Look at him, she thought wryly; he was more interested in folding his newspaper than in thinking about her.

He glanced at her again then, and Pandora's heart did an odd little somersault. The grey eyes weren't encouraging or admiring, but they held an expression that shortened her breath inexplicably and to cover her sudden confusion she lifted the hat and set it jauntily on her head.

'I think I would have worn a hat, don't you?'

It was almost a relief to see the more familiar appalled look return to his face. 'You're not seriously telling me you paid good money for *that*?'

'Don't you like it?' said Pandora innocently from somewhere beneath the rim.

'You couldn't have found something a little less excessive?'

'I feel sure that if I'd been marrying you I'd have wanted to look memorable,' she said.

'Unforgettable is one way of describing how you look now,' said Ran astringently, and Pandora had a strange feeling that he was as relieved as she at her return to normal exasperating mode. 'Totally ridiculous is another!'

She pretended to pout. 'But I bought it specially for you!'

'If you think I'm walking through the streets of Wickworth with you looking like that, you've got another think coming!'

Pandora took off the hat reluctantly and stroked its rim. 'I thought you'd like it,' she said with an exaggerated sigh of disappointment, surprising a glint of amusement in Ran's eyes as she looked up.

He dropped his paper onto the table. 'You mean you thought it would annoy me intensely?' he said, and although he didn't actually smile Pandora felt as if she'd won a great victory.

'Honest, guv, it never even crossed my mind!' she protested, putting her hand to her heart and opening her eyes wide.

His mouth twitched. 'And there was I thinking that you'd been magically transformed! It seems as if you're still the same girl underneath after all.'

'I'm afraid so,' Pandora admitted with a sigh, bending to pick up the bags which held her old clothes.

'You've still got a price tag showing,' Ran said as she straightened. 'Stand still.'

Pandora stood stock-still as he jerked the tag out of the jacket collar. She was very conscious of how close he was standing, of his hands beneath her hair, brushing against her neck. Their eyes met almost unwillingly as he stepped back, and for a moment Pandora forgot to breathe. There was a tiny pause, then Ran turned away. 'We'd better go,' he said in a brusque voice.

The atmosphere was strained as they walked back to the car to leave the bags; Pandora wanted to say something to break the silence, but she couldn't think of anything. She felt awkward and out of place in her elegant suit; even without the hat, more than one head turned to watch her pass.

They had to walk through the market to get to the photographers. Intent on not catching anyone's eye, Pandora kept her head down, and didn't notice that Ran had stopped by the flower stall until he caught her elbow. 'You need some flowers,' he said.

'Oh, I don't...' she began, but Ran was already involved in a brisk discussion with the stall-holder, as a result of·which she found her arms laden with yellow roses. Pandora buried her face in them, breathing in their heady fragrance, and smiled shyly up at Ran. 'They're lovely. Thank you.' An odd expression flickered in his eyes and she added hurriedly, 'Shouldn't you have a carnation for your buttonhole?'

'On the house,' said the stall-holder benevolently, handing a white carnation to Pandora, who then had to shift the roses onto one arm so that she had a free hand to put the carnation in Ran's buttonhole. Standing so close to him, she was overwhelmingly conscious of the strength of his body and she had to bite her lip to concentrate on slipping the stalk through the hole. In the end, Ran had to help her, his fingers deft and warm over hers.

Stricken with inexplicable shyness, Pandora felt a tide of colour rise up her cheeks as she stepped back, avoiding Ran's eyes.

'Getting married, are you?' asked the stall-holder, who had watched the little scene with interest.

'Something like that,' said Ran.

The photographer was a slender young man with artistic pretensions. He cast a doubtful glance at Pandora's hat and went into raptures about the roses and her bone structure instead as he showed them into

his studio. 'Perhaps you'd like to get ready?' he suggested to Pandora, pointing out a dressing table
equipped with brushes, tissues and a selection of make-
up before fluttering off to fuss around with the lights.

'What does he mean, "get ready"?' she asked Ran,
having recovered some of her composure. 'I *am* ready.'

'Not quite,' said Ran, picking a leaf left over from
the morning's tussle with the hedgerow from her hair.
He handed her a hairbrush. 'Most brides at least brush
their hair.'

Pandora plumped herself down at the dressing table
and gave her hair a few cursory strokes before Ran
clicked his tongue and took the brush from her firmly.
'Ow!' she protested as he tugged it through the tousled
softness until her eyes watered. 'That hurts!'

'Don't make such a fuss!' He stood back to consider
his handiwork. The dark hair fluffed around her heart-
shaped face, and he rearranged it over her shoulders,
rubbing the shining locks between his fingers almost
thoughtfully. 'There,' he said at last, turning aside to
pick up the flowers and place them back in her arms.
'*Now* you look like a girl I might fall in love with.'

Pandora stared back at him, her eyes wide and
questioning. Ran's were less easy to read, but the light
in them made the breath catch in her throat and for
some reason her heart began to thump slowly against
her ribs. He was still standing very close. . .

'Ready now?'

The photographer, bustling back, must have wondered what they had been doing, for they jerked apart
with an air that could only be described as guilty.
Pandora felt oddly jarred. She wished her breathing
would stop behaving in this bizarre way. It was only
Ran—a man who had only ever been thoroughly
disagreeable, a man who had never even smiled at

her—and she was only here because Homer had knocked over an astronomically expensive vase. That was all.

Not trusting her expression, Pandora insisted on wearing her hat, much to the dismay of the photographer, who said it would hide too much of her face. Pandora found herself defending that hat as if she really had been married in it, and compromise was only reached when Ran, impatient of the argument, proposed that there should be a couple of shots of Pandora on her own in the hat, and the rest without it. By that time she was feeling herself again and was able to agree graciously, though the light of battle still shone in her one visible eye as she tilted her face defiantly at the camera.

The photographer clearly felt that his artistic reputation was being jeopardised by Pandora's hat and was relieved when she took it off and he could place Ran next to her on the seat. 'Perhaps you could put your arms around her?' he suggested to Ran. 'And then if you just lean back against your husband, Mrs Masterson. . . Yes, that's lovely! Hold it there!'

'Relax,' muttered Ran *sotto voce* as she leant stiffly against him. 'You're supposed to be trying to be in love with me.'

'It's not that easy.' Pandora was feeling distinctly ruffled by his closeness.

'It is when you try. Just lie back and think of your debt,' he murmured in her ear. 'And don't forget to smile!'

'Are the pictures for anyone special, or just for you?' To Pandora's surprise, the photographer didn't seem to have any suspicion that they weren't in fact married.

'They're for Pandora's mother,' said Ran briefly.

'She lives in Canada,' Pandora added, mindful of the

story, and, thinking it sounded rather bald as it stood, couldn't resist embellishing it a little. 'She's bedridden so she couldn't come over for the wedding, and as she's never met Ran she naturally wants to see what he looks like.'

She could feel Ran stiffen, but the photographer was convinced. 'And a studio portrait is so much nicer than a wedding snap, isn't it?'

'Oh, we didn't have any wedding photos,' said Pandora airily. She risked a glance at Ran, who was forced to content himself with a warning look. 'We wanted our wedding to be special, with just the two of us. . .didn't we, darling?'

Ran didn't deign to answer that. 'Shall we try another shot?' was all he said, boot-faced.

In his desperation to get an 'interesting' picture, the photographer arranged them in increasingly contorted positions. Some of them were so uncomfortable that Pandora found it easier to ignore the disturbing closeness of Ran's body, and at least their joint discomfort allied them in dislike of the photographer. She could feel Ran getting more and more irritated. 'Who does he think we are?' he muttered out of the side of his mouth. 'Mr and Mrs Houdini?'

The whole situation was so absurd that Pandora began to giggle. 'Now, if you could just look into each other's eyes,' cried the photographer. Obediently, she looked at Ran, but all her efforts to look soulful and loving only made her laugh harder, and, although he tried to look disapproving, in the end Ran gave in and laughed too.

It was as if she suddenly found herself looking at a perfect stranger. Pandora's heart did a wild, breathtaking somersault at the sight of the smile creasing Ran's face, starring the lines that fanned out below his eyes

and crinkling their edges, warming the cool greyness
with amusement and illuminating his expression into
sudden clarity. Everything about him was at once
strange and utterly familiar, as if she had always known
that he would look like this when he smiled. Hadn't
she known that his teeth would be very white against
his brown skin? That his cheek would crease just like
that? Pandora could see the almost imperceptible
roughness of his jaw and her fingers tingled, almost as
if they already knew what it felt like to trace its line.

'Super!' The photographer emerged from behind his
camera and Pandora realised that her own smile was
still frozen across her face. Ran was looking at the
photographer, apparently oblivious to the dizzying
effect of his smile.

'Is that it?' he asked.

'There's just one more. What about a nice romantic
shot for your mother this time? A kiss perhaps?'

The smile flashed off Pandora's face. She didn't dare
look at Ran while he searched for an excuse.

'Good idea,' he said calmly.

Good idea? Pandora gaped at him, and he looked
back, an unreadable expression in his eyes. 'Don't you
think so, darling?' he asked, paying her back.

'Well, I. . .I don't think. . .' she floundered, but Ran
merely pulled her back along the seat towards him.

'Like this?' he asked the photographer, without
taking his eyes off Pandora.

'That's perfect!'

Ran smoothed the dark, wayward hair away from
her face, then let his hands slide, warm and gentle,
beneath it and round to caress the soft nape of her
neck while his thumbs traced the line of her jaw and
his eyes drifted over her face to rest on her mouth.

Pandora was trembling, torn between fear of what a

kiss might mean and a deep, dangerous longing, and held by the shivery promise of his thumbs caressing her skin, his fingers stroking her neck. Her heart was slamming slowly, painfully against her ribs and all the air leaked out of her lungs as she forgot to breathe, forgot the photographer, forgot everything but Ran and the quivering pulse of anticipation.

Helpless desire had deepened her eyes to a dark violet as she stared up at him, and Ran bent his head very, very slowly to touch his mouth to hers. The seat seemed to drop away beneath Pandora as the studio tilted and swung giddily around her, and she gasped involuntarily at that first electrifying touch of his lips.

How could she have thought of his mouth as cool? It was warm—warm and sure and persuasive. All sensation arrowed to the feel of it against hers, and nothing mattered but the rush of intoxicating pleasure as she leant instinctively into the kiss. Her hands rose of their own accord to his wrists, but instead of pulling them away her fingers clutched at him in unspoken need, and the pressure of his lips increased as if in response.

And then he was drawing away, and his hands were drifting down her throat. For a long moment he held her like that as he looked deep into her dazed eyes, before releasing her with a twisted smile.

CHAPTER THREE

'YOUR mum'll love that one,' said the photographer with satisfaction.

At the thought of her mother's reaction if she were sent a photograph of her daughter kissing a perfect stranger, Pandora had to fight a bubble of hysterical laughter. She felt very peculiar. As if from a great distance, she could hear Ran discussing details about contact sheets and collection times, and wondered with a twinge of resentment how he could sound so *normal* when that kiss had left her feeling feverish and disembodied.

She looked around the studio, at Ran and the photographer talking together, and none of it seemed real. Real was the warmth of his mouth, the tingling touch of his hands, the swamping rush of sheer pleasure. Her body was still throbbing with it, her lips still afire, and when she looked down at her fingers it was as if she could still feel the short hairs on his wrist where she had held him.

Somehow she must have said goodbye, for the next thing Pandora knew she was standing on the pavement outside with Ran, blinking at the sunshine and clutching her hat beneath the armful of roses. A fresh breeze whipped her hair around, but she had no free hand to brush it away, and when Ran looked at her her face was almost totally obscured by the tousled cloud. He sighed.

'You've only been outside for thirty seconds and already you look a mess!'

Pandora tried to toss the hair out of her eyes. 'It's hard to look neat when a gale's blowing,' she protested, although she noticed that Ran managed to do so without any difficulty. The wind was barely ruffling his short brown hair and he looked as solid and orderly as ever. Everything about him was so *definite*, she thought. Where she carried a vaguely chaotic air around with her, always on the verge of tangling her legs together, Ran was totally controlled. It was obvious in the easy, deliberate way he moved, the way he spoke, the way he glanced at his watch.

The way he kissed.

Pandora stared fixedly down at the roses, glad now of the hair that hid her face.

'Let's go and have some lunch,' he said.

He took her to a quiet little restaurant tucked away behind the market square. Pandora escaped almost immediately to the Ladies, ostensibly to brush her hair but in fact to try and pull herself together. When she looked in the mirror, her eyes were huge and dark beneath the tangle of hair, but otherwise she was astonished to see how normal she looked. She had expected to see her mouth still red and throbbing from his kiss and her cheeks aflame with the blood that was still churning along her veins.

She ran her hands under cold water and pressed them to her face. It was silly to react like this. Anyone would think she had never been kissed before. It hadn't even been a real kiss! How long had it lasted? Thirty seconds? A minute?

An eternity, a voice inside her answered before Pandora squashed it firmly. She had better things to do than work herself up into a state about a stupid kiss, no matter *how* long it had lasted. It was just part of the pretence that would enable Ran to leave Kendrick Hall as soon as possible and go back to Africa. The sooner the better, Pandora told herself. Then she could go back to her pottery and forget about how warm his mouth had been, how unexpected his smile.

In the meantime, she would go back to the table and pretend that she wasn't in the slightest bit bothered by the fact that he had kissed her. If Ran could behave as if nothing had happened, so could she!

Pandora was proud of the cool way she accepted the menu he handed her as she sat down. He had taken off his jacket, and the plain white shirt made him look tougher and more tanned than ever. She studied him covertly over the top of the menu. His eyes were lowered as his read his own, brows drawn together slightly, and her gaze drifted of its own accord down the straight nose to that cool, exciting mouth.

Why did she have to look at his mouth? Pandora jerked her eyes away, but one look had been enough to set the memory of how it had felt against hers strumming inside her, and the set of his lips continued to dance before her as she gazed blindly at the menu. What was it about him that gave her this strange, fluttery feeling inside? He had only ever been cold and cross and disagreeable, and she didn't think it was anything to do with looks. Ran wasn't smooth enough to be strictly handsome. There was a rough edge to him, something forceful and individual about his features that made handsome too weak a word for him. He was too cool, too tough, too self-contained.

Pandora couldn't quite put her finger on what it was that was so different about him. It might have been something to do with that quality of restrained competence that seemed so typical of him, or the sense of massive, understated strength that set him apart from every other man in the room. After all, they all had two eyes, a nose and a mouth. . .it was just that none of them had a mouth that turned her bones to water whenever she thought about it.

You're not suppo_ed to be thinking about his mouth, Pandora told herself desperately. You're behaving as if nothing happened, remember? She tried to concentrate on the menu, but her gaze kept sliding surreptitiously round the side and over the top to rest on his hands, his hair, the bridge of his nose.

Snapping his menu shut without warning, Ran looked up to find Pandora's eyes on him. She had forgotten just how acute his grey eyes could be, and a tide of colour seeped into her cheeks. He raised an eyebrow at her expression. 'Have you decided?'

'Decided?' she repeated blankly.

'What you'd like to eat,' he explained with exaggerated patience.

'Oh, yes. . .' Pandora cast a wild eye over the menu, but the print kept wavering over the page. She *must* pull herself together! 'I'll. . .er. . .have the chicken.' Chicken was the first word she could decipher, and she would just have to discover in what form it came.

'Are you all right, Pandora?' Ran asked when he had given the order to the waiter.

'I'm fine,' she said quickly.

'You just seem rather distracted—or is that normal for you?'

Pandora fiddled with her napkin and wished he weren't quite so perceptive. 'I've got a lot on my mind,' she said discouragingly, but Ran was not deterred.

'What sort of things?'

'Well. . .the exhibition for a start. I've never had my own exhibition before, so I want to do well. I've only got two more weeks to get everything ready. I can't really afford to take all this time off.'

'You can't really afford to buy a new Chinese vase either, can you, Pandora?'

'No.' She should have known better than to expect any sympathy from Ran.

'Where is this exhibition going to be?'

'At the gallery in the market square.'

He frowned. 'You set that up pretty quickly, didn't you? I thought you hadn't been here long?'

'About six weeks,' said Pandora, sitting back so that the waiter could pour her a glass of wine. 'The gallery was originally going to have an exhibition of Celia's work—she's a potter too—but she and John were sent to the States at short notice.

'After I left art college I didn't have anywhere to work. I used various friends' studios for a while and then Celia suggested that I use hers while she and John were away. It was all so perfect,' she went on wistfully, running her finger round the rim of her glass. 'Living here for free means that I can concentrate on my pottery. I'd never be able to afford to do it otherwise, and when Celia introduced me to the gallery owner and suggested that I should have her slot. . .well, it was too good to be true.'

Ran took a sip of his wine and watched Pandora's face over the glass, his expression inscrutable. 'One day spent acting as my wife isn't going to ruin the exhibition, is it?'

She hesitated. How could she tell him that it wasn't so much the time spent with him as the concentration lost and the time wasted thinking about him? 'No,' she said reluctantly.

'In that case, we'd better make up some story about how we met in case Myra and Elaine ask,' said Ran briskly, having evidently disposed of the exhibition as a major problem. 'Have you ever been to Africa?'

Pandora was thrown by the sudden change of subject. 'I've been to Italy,' she offered.

'Italy's not quite Africa, is it?'

'Well, it's the best I can do,' she said grumpily, still piqued by his lack of interest in her exhibition. OK, Wickworth wasn't exactly a renowned artistic centre, but it was a start.

'Hmm.' Ran frowned down into his glass. 'What about your family? Have any of them ever been there?'

She shook her head. 'Dad's a vicar, and we always had our family holidays in Scotland. Why do we have to have met in Africa, anyway? Why don't we just tell them the truth?'

'What, that I caught you and your dog smashing a priceless family heirloom?'

Pandora lifted her chin. 'At least we wouldn't have any trouble remembering the story. We don't need to say when it happened.'

'Unfortunately Myra and Elaine already know that I've only been at Kendrick Hall for a week. People don't get married in a matter of days, do they?'

'We could have fallen in love at first sight,' said Pandora, reluctant to give up.

'We could, but we didn't, did we?'

She thought of how she had first seen him: tall, powerful, blazingly angry. 'Of course not,' she said in a flat voice.

'Anyway,' Ran went on, 'I've already told them you've been in Africa with me. We'll have to make something up. Have you got any brothers and sisters?'

'Two brothers. Ben's still at school and Harry's just qualified as an engineer. He's working in London at the moment.'

'Harry will do fine. For our purposes he can be

working in Africa. We'll tell Myra and Elaine that we met when you came out to visit him.'

'But what if they ask me what it was like? I've never *been* to Africa.'

'Nor, I should imagine, have Myra and Elaine. You must have seen some safari documentaries on television. All you have to do is sound vague, and you shouldn't find *that* much of a problem!'

Pandora eyed him with some hostility. 'All right, so we've been living in Africa, and came back to England when we heard you'd inherited Kendrick Hall?'

'And now we're both very enthusiastic about the idea of entertaining American guests,' Ran finished for her. 'It's not exactly a complicated plot. Do you think you'll be able to remember it?'

'I'm sure it won't be as easy as that,' said Pandora gloomily. 'They're bound to ask me something I haven't a clue about, like whether you like sprouts or how you get on with my mother.'

'They're hardly likely to cross-examine you,' he said with a touch of impatience. 'If they ask you anything you don't know, you'll have to make it up.'

'It would still help if I knew *something* about you.'

Ran looked impatient. 'What do you want to know?'

How it would feel if she leant across the table and laid her palm against his cheek. What it would be like to be able to smile at him and know that he would smile back. Whether she would ever be able to forget the way he had kissed her.

'Oh, just things,' said Pandora, avoiding his eye. 'When your birthday is, whether you've got any brothers and sisters, whether you've always been bad-tempered—that kind of thing.'

'I'm not in the least bad-tempered,' said Ran bad-temperedly. 'At least, I wasn't until I saw thirty thousand pounds smash onto the floor,' he amended when Pandora choked over her wine.

'I might have known it would be my fault!'

'All right, until I inherited Kendrick Hall,' he allowed a little ungraciously as the waiter placed their plates before them.

Pandora picked up her knife and fork, only slightly mollified. 'Most people would be delighted to inherit a lovely old house like that.'

'What's the point of a house you can't live in?' he asked. 'Quite apart from anything else, it's far too big for a single man.'

She concentrated on her chicken. 'You might have a family one day.'

'No.' Ran was curt to the point of rudeness, and from his expression Pandora judged it best to steer the conversation away from families. What did she care anyway if he never wanted a wife or children?

'It would still be a lovely house to live in,' she said, thinking of the rambling stone house whose wings had been added in a haphazard fashion over the centuries to the original medieval hall. 'It always looks so romantic, practically reeking of history.'

'It certainly reeks of damp,' said Ran prosaically. 'Have you any idea how much it's going to cost to restore?'

'Thirty thousand pounds?'

He glanced at her sharply, but Pandora was sipping her wine and looking innocent. 'That would cover the main problems, but it's going to need a lot more work before I can start charging people to stay there. You might think Kendrick Hall is romantic, but as far as I'm concerned it's just an expensive burden. It's not as if the house even means anything to me. I'd never even been there before last week.'

'Didn't your uncle ever invite you to stay?' said Pandora, surprised, and he gave a mirthless laugh.

'As far as my uncle was concerned, my father was the black sheep of the family. He wouldn't even have his name mentioned and refused to have anything to do with me even when I was over here at boarding-school and university.'

'He must have changed his mind if he left you the house.'

'He didn't have any choice about that. The estate's entailed to the nearest male relative and Eustace didn't have any children.'

Pandora chewed on her chicken. 'So what will happen if you don't have any children?'

His face closed. 'That won't be my problem.'

'Don't you have any brothers either?' she asked, feeling as if she had been tactless.

'No, I was an only child.'

'Weren't you ever lonely?' said Pandora, who couldn't imagine what her life would have been like without brothers to fight and play and argue with.

Ran shrugged. 'I was brought up in Ghana. When I was small I used to play with the local children, so I never missed having brothers and sisters. Africa is much more my home than Kendrick Hall will ever be.'

'And you've never married?' she steeled herself to ask.

'What is this—an interrogation?' he said, annoyed.

'I'm only trying to find out something about you,' said Pandora huffily. 'How can I pretend to be your wife unless I know some basic facts? I'd have thought whether you'd ever been married or not was quite a pretty basic thing to know about one's husband.'

'It is if you're going to spend the rest of your life

with someone. We're only going to spend twenty-four hours together.'

'Why are you being so cagey about it?' she demanded.

'I am not being *cagey*.' A muscle was beginning to beat irritably in Ran's jaw. 'Since you're so interested, no, I have never been married, and I fully intend to remain that way. I have an open and undemanding relationship with an American woman who also works in Mbuzi—a relationship which both of us are content to leave exactly as it is. Now, is there anything else you want to know about my private life or can we carry on with our lunch?'

'What's her name?' Pandora was unable to resist asking.

He sighed. 'Cindy.'

Cindy? What a stupid name! Pandora glowered down at her plate. Trust Ran to like a girl with a name like that. She was probably sugary and sweet and agreed with everything he said. 'What's she like?' she asked, although she wasn't really sure she wanted to know.

'She's very bright, smart, capable and extremely nice,' said Ran, obviously comparing her with Pandora who didn't seem to fit into any of those categories.

'I suppose she's pretty too,' she said sulkily.

'Very.'

'Oh.' Pandora was definitely wishing she hadn't asked now, but it was a bit late now. 'How did you meet her? Did her dog run amok in your house?'

'If Cindy had a dog she would doubtless keep it well under control,' he said with a repressive look. 'Actually, she works for one of the big aid agencies. She's extremely good at her job.'

Pandora stabbed at a piece of chicken. 'If she's so wonderful, why isn't she here with you?'

'She's gone home to the States on leave. In any case, we don't have that sort of relationship. Cindy's career-orientated and she knows that I'm not interested in marriage. We enjoy ourselves when we're together but neither of us want to get involved with ties or commitments.'

'You can't be in love with each other, then,' said Pandora crossly. She didn't want to think about why she was so cross. It was probably her disturbed night catching up with her, and nothing whatsoever to do with the perfection of Ran's girlfriend.

Ran glared at her across the table. He looked just as cross as she felt. 'How I feel about Cindy is none of your business,' he snapped. 'I thought you just wanted to ask about my birthday, not analyse my relationships.'

'All right, when's your birthday?' she said, pushing some rice sulkily around her plate.

'April the twenty-seventh.' He held up a mocking hand. 'Don't tell me! I'm a Leo or a Gemini or something.'

'Taurus, actually,' said Pandora coldly.

'I thought you would know.' Ran didn't even bother to hide his sneer. 'You arty types are always into that kind of nonsense, aren't you? I suppose you're going to analyse my star sign now.'

Pandora put down her fork with a click. 'I don't need to,' she said. 'I already know we're not compatible!'

They glared at each other across the table. Ran was looking forbidding, while Pandora took a defiant slug of her wine, her eyes very violet and her chin tilted at a challenging angle.

The taut silence was broken by a voice speaking Pandora's name with a note of query. 'Pandora?'

Absorbed in the quarrel with Ran which seemed to have sprung up out of nowhere, Pandora looked blank

at first, then her brow cleared as she recognised the
man standing by their table, looking as if he wasn't
quite sure whether he recognised her or not. He was
tall and fair, with suave good looks and a patrician air.

'Hello, Quentin.'

'It *is* you,' he said, looking her over with blatant
admiration. 'For a minute there I wasn't sure! You
look fabulous!'

Out of the corner of her eye, Pandora saw Ran's
brows snap together and she smiled so brilliantly up at
Quentin that he blinked. 'Why, thank you!' she said
sweetly.

She wasn't surprised that he had had trouble recognising her. The only other time they had met had been
when Celia had taken her into the gallery to introduce
her and she had been wearing torn jeans and a faded
T-shirt she often used to work in. Quentin hadn't been
overly impressed but he had been persuaded by Celia
and the samples of her work to give her a chance at an
exhibition. Now he was looking at her as if the ugly
duckling had been unexpectedly transformed into a
swan, and, thinking that it wouldn't do Ran any harm
to see that she wasn't in the least jealous of perfect
Cindy, Pandora lifted her cheek for a kiss.

Quentin obliged with obvious pleasure while Ran
watched, concrete-faced. 'How are things going?' he
asked with far more interest than he had shown when
he had met her before. 'Are you going to have everything ready for the exhibition?'

'I hope so. I've got one or two minor distractions at
the moment,' said Pandora, peeping under her lashes
at Ran. A tell-tale muscle was twitching in his temple.
'But don't worry, it's nothing important—'

'Aren't you going to introduce us, *darling*?' Ran
interrupted in a harsh voice.

Pandora glowered at him. She didn't in the least want to introduce the two men, but she didn't have much alternative now. 'Quentin Moss, Ran Masterson,' she said with bad grace. 'Quentin owns the gallery which is putting on my exhibition,' she added, but deliberately didn't explain who Ran was.

The two men shook hands without enthusiasm, eyeing each other up like circling dogs. Quentin had evidently registered both Ran's 'darling' and Pandora's glare, for he turned back to her almost immediately. 'We must have lunch,' he said in a warmly caressing voice. 'I haven't seen nearly enough of you, and I did promise Celia I'd look after you, didn't I? Why don't you come in one day next week? We can go over the arrangements for the exhibition and then go on to a little restaurant I know.'

'You're rather busy next week, aren't you, Pandora?' Ran put in with a warning look.

Pandora thought of Cindy. 'I'm sure I can squeeze Quentin in somewhere,' she said, returning his look with a stubborn tilt of her chin before smiling up at Quentin. 'What about Monday?'

'Super.' He bent to kiss her cheek again with a triumphant look at Ran. 'I'll look forward to it.'

Pandora smiled prettily at him, one eye on Ran's expression. She felt quite exhilarated. If she had known a suit could have this effect, she would have worn one before!

Ran opened his mouth to give her a piece of his mind, only to close it again as the waiter approached to remove their plates. The frustration didn't improve his temper. '"I'm sure I can squeeze Quentin in somewhere,"' he mimicked her savagely as soon as the waiter had disappeared.

Pandora opened her eyes wide. 'Is there a problem?' she asked sweetly.

'You may have forgotten about the thirty thousand pounds you owe me, but I haven't!' he grated. 'You're supposed to be being my wife next week!'

'Only for twenty-four hours,' she reminded him. 'I can't see that it makes any difference to you what I do for the rest of the week.'

'And what happens if Myra and Elaine decide to turn up on Monday?' he said nastily. 'How are you going to *squeeze in* lover boy then?'

'I'm sure I'll be able to arrange to meet him another day.' They faced each other angrily. 'What do you care what I do, anyway? I thought all you cared about was getting back to your precious Cindy?'

'I won't be able to do that if you don't play your part convincingly next week,' snapped Ran. 'And you're going to have to do better than today's performance if you want to convince Myra and Elaine that you're my wife and not that smarmy art dealer's!'

'I didn't realise I was on duty yet,' said Pandora tartly.

'Considering that you're wearing a suit I've bought and eating a lunch I'm paying for, I think it might have crossed your mind, don't you?'

Pandora opened her pudding menu furiously. 'Do you calculate how much you've spent on Cindy too? Some "open" relationship!'

'Leave Cindy out of this!'

'I will if you'll leave Quentin out of it!'

'Why are you concerned about him all of a sudden?' demanded Ran. 'He wouldn't have taken any notice of you if I hadn't dressed you up in those clothes.'

'You don't know that.' Pandora shut the menu with

a vicious smack. 'Just because you're not interested in me doesn't mean that nobody else is.'

'I'm more surprised that you could be interested in him,' he sneered. 'Surely you're not really impressed by that slimy, sophisticated act?' He muttered under his breath as the waiter materialised once more, 'You don't want any pudding, do you?'

'I'll have the chocolate truffle cake, please,' said Pandora, who had just decided that she didn't want anything. She directed a blinding smile at the waiter and waited until he had taken Ran's order for coffee before she went back on the attack. 'And Quentin is not slimy! He *is* sophisticated, but I couldn't expect you to recognise sophistication when you saw it. He's also charming and cultured and considerate—unlike some people I could mention!'

Ran snorted. 'Culture and consideration? Is that all you want from a man?'

'It's obviously more than Cindy does!'

'Cindy's far too sensible to waste her time dreaming about the sort of man who'd slip through your fingers if you tried to pick him up,' said Ran unpleasantly. 'I hadn't credited you with much sense, I know, but I thought you'd have more than that!'

Pandora's smile was brittle. 'Well, we arty types have to stick together, don't we? And another thing—I'd appreciate it if you didn't refer to me as "darling" again!'

'I think the least you owe me is a few "darlings",' he pointed out with a saturnine look.

'Homer only broke one vase,' Pandora reminded him sullenly. 'You can call me "darling" in Kendrick Hall when the Americans are there; that's all I agreed. It's all right for you. You're going back to Africa, but

I've got to spend the whole year here. How am I going to explain to Quentin who you are?'

'Tell him that I'm a jealous lover.'

Her heart had only just got back to normal. Now the mere idea of Ran as a lover sent it flipping up to lodge in her throat again. If only she couldn't imagine it quite so vividly: Ran pulling her slowly into his arms, Ran undoing the zip of her dress, Ran smiling, his hands sliding over her body. . .

'And what am I supposed to tell him when you've gone?' Pandora's voice sounded high and constricted.

'You can say that I've left you,' he suggested.

'Thanks! That *will* impress Quentin!'

'If he really cares about you, he'll be so glad to have you to himself that he won't care one way or another,' said Ran indifferently, and Pandora subsided into sullen silence.

Having insisted on a pudding, she had to plough her way through the chocolate truffle cake while Ran stirred his coffee broodingly. She told herself that she was glad that he had shown himself to be such a selfish, arrogant, unreasonable pig. It was much easier to quarrel with him than to remember the feel of his lips and the touch of his hands and the way he had looked when he'd smiled. She just wished she could get rid of that vision of him pulling her into his arms. It simmered tantalisingly at the edge of her mind, beckoning her imagination in spite of every attempt to recall how unpleasant he had been.

Pandora pushed her plate aside and risked a glance at him, hoping that he would suddenly have turned into an innocuous stranger. Of course it *would* be just as he looked up from his coffee. Violet eyes jarred with grey before both looked quickly away. The look had lasted only a matter of seconds, but it had been enough to change the atmosphere from sulky antagonism to a new kind of strained silence that was less identifiable and infinitely more uncomfortable.

No, there was nothing innocuous about Ran Masterson.

They drove home in the same uneasy silence. It had been easier when they'd been arguing, Pandora decided, looking out of her window and trying not to notice how brown and capable his hands looked on the steering wheel, the same hands that she had imagined sliding her dress from her shoulders—

She had to stop this! It was the silence that was unnerving her, that was all. Pandora jerked bolt upright in her seat and sought desperately for something to say. 'Do I have to do anything else before the Americans arrive?' The squeaky voice didn't sound at all like her own.

'You can decide on what you're going to cook.' Ran didn't look away from the road. 'I'll let you know as soon as they tell me when they're coming, and then I can take you shopping for anything you need.'

'I can drive myself,' said Pandora.

'You're the one who keeps going on about how busy you are,' he said. 'I'm sure it will be quicker if I go with you. At least then you won't be tempted into a time-consuming detour into the art gallery.'

Pandora folded her arms crossly. 'Suit yourself.'

'I will,' he assured her.

He dropped her at the entrance to the stables, and didn't even bother to turn the engine off while she got out. 'I'll leave you to plan the menu,' he said sardonically, and drove off down the avenue towards the Hall, leaving Pandora staring resentfully after him.

CHAPTER FOUR

IT WAS two days before she saw him again. Pandora tried to forget him by throwing herself into her pottery, but it wasn't any good. The memory of that brief, meaningless, *stupid* kiss lurked infuriatingly, ready to spring out and ambush her just when she thought that she had succeeded in putting Ran Masterson completely out of her mind.

Walking Homer, making a cup of tea, brushing her teeth. . .it didn't matter what she was doing; his face would shimmer suddenly behind her eyelids, and something warm and feverish and infinitely disturbing would stir inside her. Pandora felt restless and unsettled. She kept putting down what she was doing and starting on something else, until the house was littered with unfinished jobs and she began to get cross.

It wasn't fair. It was only a kiss. She didn't even like the man. Why couldn't she put him out of her mind and concentrate on her exhibition instead of thinking about how unnerving his touch had been? Pandora put away the mug she had just got out to make a cup of tea and slammed the cupboard shut. She was going to make some more bowls and she was not—absolutely, definitely *not*—going to think about Ran Masterson.

Outside, the afternoon sun slanted across the cobbled courtyard as she walked barefoot across to the studio. Propping the door open to let in the drifting scent of honeysuckle and the lavender Celia had planted by the wall, Pandora wedged up some clay and whacked the first ball onto the wheel. She was wearing a loose long-sleeved top over a cheesecloth skirt, which meant that she had to keep stopping to push up her sleeves to stop them trailing, but she didn't care. The hypnotic rhythm of the wheel and the smoothness of the clay between her wet hands was soothingly familiar and gradually she relaxed, letting the shape and the feel of the clay absorb her.

Homer had found one of her discarded sandals in the kitchen and lay chewing it nearby. He was happy because Pandora had spent much of the last two days trying to walk off the odd, unsettled feeling she had been left with after the trip to Wickworth with Ran. Pandora didn't even notice that he had her shoe. She was humming tunelessly to herself, adrift in a world of her own where the clay took shape miraculously beneath her hands.

Before long she had nearly completed a tray-load and was easing another bowl into shape, her hair pushed haphazardly behind her ears and her legs tucked under the seat, like a little girl. The sun was streaming through the open window beside her, enveloping her in a warm aura of light that burnished the soft cloud of her hair and tipped the ends of her lashes with gold. Oblivious to her surroundings, Pandora's expression was serenely absorbed as she dipped her hands in water and slid them up the sides of the clay.

A fist banging on the door jerked her head round. The sight of Ran framed in the open doorway jarred her heart and her hands slipped, ruining the bowl, which slumped back into a shapeless lump of clay. Homer, roused from eyebrow-twitching slumber, scrambled to his feet and began to bark furiously to cover his embarrassment at having been caught unawares.

The noise gave Pandora a chance to get her lurching

heart under control. Just when she had persuaded herself that she hadn't really been bothered by that kiss after all, Ran had to come and ruin everything. He was dressed in khaki trousers and a short-sleeved white shirt which emphasised his bronzed skin, and he looked crisp and cool and utterly unnerving. Pandora might tell herself what she liked, but she hadn't forgotten a single detail about him, and he was still able to drive the breath from her lungs just by standing there.

'Hello.' She stood up, horrified by how squeaky her voice sounded.

Ran had succeeded in calming Homer's first excitement. 'Not much of a guard dog, is he?' he said caustically by way of a greeting. 'I've been standing here for five minutes waiting for one of you to notice me.'

'You should have said something.' Pandora had cleared her throat and she sounded almost normal this time.

'I did.' There was an odd note in his voice as if he was remembering how she had looked in the warm afternoon sunshine. 'You were miles away.'

For some reason, Pandora felt a slow flush start at her toes and tingle upwards at the thought of his eyes on her, and she turned away to busy herself rinsing her hands. 'I was thinking about what I was doing,' she said. He needn't think she'd been wasting any time thinking about *him*!

'Homer wasn't,' said Ran austerely, but rather spoiled the effect by bending to pat the dog, who was still showing a quite unjustified pleasure in seeing him. 'You'd think he'd be good for something, wouldn't you?'

'He's good at lots of things,' said Pandora, leaping to Homer's defence.

'Oh, yes? Like what? Trespassing? Breaking other people's property?'

She ignored that. Wiping her hands on her skirt, she tried to think of one thing Homer could do that might impress Ran. 'He runs after sticks.'

'Ah, but does he bring them back?'

Pandora put up her chin. 'Sometimes,' she said defiantly but untruthfully.

'Very handy.' Ran's expression was sardonic. He prowled around the studio as if restless himself, stopping at the workbench to pick up one of her finished pieces—a vast fruit bowl decorated with a riot of tropical plants, with monkeys peeking through palm leaves and brightly coloured parrots. 'Did you make this?' he asked in surprise.

'It's one of the pieces for the exhibition,' she said, gesturing along the bench, which was crammed with jugs, bowls, mugs, vases, plates and dishes. All were decorated with different, unusual designs, but Pandora's distinctive style was obvious.

Ran turned the bowl thoughtfully between his hands and looked at her as if he had never seen her before. 'It's. . .original,' he said, then hesitated. 'I hadn't realised you were this good,' he added frankly.

Pandora was furious with herself for the thrill of pleasure his admission gave her. She shifted some mugs needlessly around the bench. 'Thank you,' she muttered without looking at him.

'How long have you been doing this?' he asked, putting down the bowl and picking up a milk jug painted with a lugubrious cow. He was only a couple of feet away and Pandora moved—casually, she hoped—further away from the disturbing power of his body.

'I first saw Celia throwing a pot when I was nine,' she said. 'She put this lump of clay on the wheel and under her hands it turned into this wonderful shape right before my eyes.' She looked out of the window at the sun throwing shadows across the courtyard and she smiled, her eyes dreamy with the remembered excitement of that moment. 'I thought it was. . .magical. Ever since then, pottery has been all I've ever wanted to do.'

Turning her head, she surprised a peculiar expression in Ran's eyes, but they shuttered so quickly that she thought she must have imagined it. He put the jug carefully back down on the bench. 'All?' he said. 'I thought you girls spent your time yearning for weddings and babies?'

Pandora stiffened at the dismissive tone of his voice. He had an unsettling habit of tempting her into thinking that he might be quite nice after all, only to turn round and say something that made her realise that actually he was just as disagreeable as ever.

'I haven't got anything against weddings or babies,' she said, as coolly as she could. 'But I'm not going to think about either until I've found the right man.'

'What sort of man is that, Pandora?' Ran leant back against the bench, crossing his legs at the ankle and putting his hands into his trouser pockets. In spite of his relaxed posture, there was a coiled quality about him, as if he was just waiting to pounce. It made Pandora nervous.

'I don't think I'll know until I've found him,' she said uneasily.

'Oh, come on,' he said, deliberately provocative. 'You can't tell me you've been so wrapped up in your pottery that you've never given it any thought. You must have some idea.'

'Well, he won't be anyone like you!' snapped Pandora, unaccountably ruffled. 'All I'm looking for is someone who loves me enough not to be satisfied with any open relationship!'

'Someone like Quentin Moss?' he asked with a contemptuous look, and Pandora, who hadn't given Quentin so much as a thought since leaving the restaurant the other day and would have been hard pressed to describe what he looked like, shook back her hair defiantly.

'Maybe,' she said, her violet eyes bright with challenge.

Ran's expression of distaste deepened. 'I wouldn't place too many hopes on him if I were you,' he said unpleasantly. 'He struck me as a man who didn't love anyone but himself.'

'It takes one to know one!' she flashed, and turned away to dump the unused clay back into the pugging mill. She would never be able to do any work now!

'Just warning you for your own good,' said Ran, unperturbed, and Pandora slammed the lid of the mill shut.

'Did you want something?' she asked in a cold voice.

'I've heard from Myra,' he said, suddenly brisk. 'They're coming on Tuesday, about teatime, which means we'll have to do the shopping on Monday.'

'Why can't we do it on Tuesday morning?'

'Because you're going to be too busy on Tuesday morning getting everything ready,' said Ran, reverting to his usual irritable manner. 'You'll just have to cancel your date with your arty friend.'

Pandora had forgotten about lunch with Quentin, but now that Ran had reminded her she was utterly determined to go. 'It's not as if we're going to have to withstand a siege,' she pointed out. 'It won't take us all day to shop for a couple of meals. I'll have plenty of time to meet Quentin afterwards.'

Ran scowled. 'Am I supposed to wait around until you've finished?'

She was delighted at having found a way to thwart him. It seemed to make up in part for the long hours she had wasted trying not to think about him. 'I wouldn't dream of putting you to so much trouble,' she assured him sweetly. 'I can go in my van.'

'What, in that old rust bucket sitting outside?' he exclaimed in disgust. 'Surely that's not allowed on the roads?'

'It passed its MOT,' said Pandora, stung. She was fond of her old van, which Harry had bought for her at an auction. True, it wasn't the most reliable vehicle on the road, but they couldn't all have big new four-wheel drives like Ran Masterson, could they?

Ran's jaw was working in exasperation. 'It's ridiculous to go in two vehicles,' he said at last. 'Since you're so insistent about going out to lunch, I'll take you in and drop you at the gallery. I've got various things I need to do in town, so I can get through some business then pick you up and we can do the shopping on the way home.'

'Thereby ensuring that I have to cut lunch with Quentin short,' Pandora commented with an uncharacteristic edge to her voice, and his frown deepened.

'Look, after Tuesday you can spend all day and all night with Quentin as far as I'm concerned,' he said brutally. 'All I care about is making the Americans' visit a successful one. When that's over we can forget each other, but in the meantime I'm prepared to do whatever's necessary to convince them that not only do I have a wife, but also a suitable one. Which reminds me...' He turned to pick up an envelope he had dropped on the table when he'd first come in and tossed it across to Pandora. 'I'm about to go and order one of these photographs to be blown up and framed. Have a look at these.'

Pandora's defiant attitude wilted somewhat at the mention of the photographs. It brought back too many memories she would have preferred to keep firmly forgotten. She sat down at the table and drew the contact sheet out of the envelope gingerly, as if it were liable to explode in her face.

It might as well have done. The photographs brought back that wretched kiss with a jolting rush and she was glad that she was sitting down. There she was, looking challenging in that absurd hat, leaning back against Ran, laughing with him. Kissing him. It was as if she could still feel the tingling warmth of his hands, the tantalising touch of his mouth.

Pandora jerked her eyes away from that particular shot, but it might as well have been surrounded with flashing lights for all she could ignore it. The sight of her mouth touching Ran's kept tugging at the edge of her vision, and made her heart boom and thud with remembered feeling. Had they really looked so natural together, so *right*? The other photographs were nearly as disquieting. In most of them, Ran was looking down at her tenderly while her own expression was soft and shining.

We look as if we're in love, she thought, and her heart did a giddy flip, to land with an ominous thud somewhere in the depths of her stomach.

'Quite convincing, aren't they?' said Ran, as if reading her thoughts.

'Quite.' Pandora swallowed. 'Wh-which one are you going to have blown up?'

He leant over her shoulder, frazzling her nerves even further, and indicated first the shot the photographer had caught of them laughing together and then the one of the kiss. 'I thought one of those two.'

'That one,' said Pandora quickly, pointing to the one of them laughing.

'I knew you'd say that,' said Ran in a dry voice. To her relief, he took the contact sheet and moved away to put it back in the envelope. 'Personally, I thought the kiss looked very effective.' He shot her one of his quick, sharp glances. 'No one seeing a photograph would guess that we weren't really in love, would they?'

'Do you think so?' Pandora willed herself to sound casual. 'I just think the shot of us laughing looks more natural.' She got to her feet, careful to avoid Ran's eyes. 'The kiss was so contrived that I'd have thought it was obvious that it wasn't a real kiss, that's all.'

'Wasn't it?' There was a disturbing undercurrent of amusement in his voice. 'It felt pretty real to me!'

Pandora folded her arms in front of her in a gesture that managed to be cross, defiant and defensive all at the same time. 'You know what I mean!'

'Yes, I know exactly what you mean, Pandora,' Ran said ironically as he moved towards the door. 'I'll leave you to your art. Just make sure you've got a shopping list ready for Monday. I'm not going to spend the entire afternoon dithering in the supermarket. Have you decided what you're going to cook yet?'

'Can't I just buy something ready-made?' pleaded Pandora.

'No, you can't. They're going to be expecting good, home-cooked food, and a decent meal could be just what's required to swing their opinion in our favour.'

'But I hate cooking,' she protested. 'The ingredients never do what I want them to do. I'll never be able to manage a grand dinner party.'

An impatient expression crossed Ran's face. 'Surely it's just a matter of following a simple recipe?'

'Recipes are never simple,' said Pandora glumly. 'There's always some vital ingredient left out, or you have to use some piece of equipment that you pay a fortune for, only to use once. Besides,' she went on, 'why should women always be expected to do the cooking? Why can't *you* do it? I'm sure that would impress Myra and Elaine.'

'*I* can't cook!'

Pandora widened her eyes at him. 'Surely it's just a matter of following a simple recipe?' she reminded him sweetly, and his eyes narrowed.

'This isn't a commission for sexual equality,' he said sourly. 'I'm not doing the cooking because *I'm* not responsible for breaking a thirty thousand-pound vase and you are. It's as simple as that.' Without giving her a chance to retort, he turned and walked out, but he put his head back round the door briefly to remind her of their next meeting. 'I'll pick you up at eleven o'clock on Monday. Please be ready and waiting.'

'"Please be ready and waiting,"' Pandora mimicked furiously to Homer when he had gone, and kicked a crumpled scrap of paper across the floor. Why was it that Ran always managed to twist her up into knots, leaving her cross and edgy and thoroughly confused about *what* she felt?

Sighing, she collapsed back down onto a chair. If only he weren't so hard to ignore. If only she weren't so aware of him, of the way he looked and the way he moved and the way he had felt and touched and tasted.

If only he hadn't kissed her.

She had been through all this before! Pandora forced herself back to the wheel, but the tranquillity she had

found earlier had vanished. Her senses jangled as if
Ran's presence still vibrated in the air and the photographs kept flickering through her mind as a series of
disturbingly vivid images. It had been odd to see herself
looking so relaxed and happy with Ran. Odd and
unsettling and yet somehow familiar. Really, she must
be a better actress than either of them had suspected.

By the time Monday came, Pandora had herself well
under control. She was sick of thinking about Ran
Masterson. How could a man she had only met four times
have become the focus of her life? It was absolutely
ridiculous. The whole affair was nearly over. All she
had to do was get through the next day, and then she
and Ran would be able to go their own ways. He would
go back to Africa and his perfect open relationship
with Cindy and she would never need to see him again.

'Good,' said Pandora out loud to Celia's tubs of
geraniums. She was watering them while she waited for
Ran to arrive. It was another hot, sunny day and the
cobbles were already warm beneath her bare feet.
Homer had had an early walk in the cool, and was
already shut in the kitchen so that Ran would have no
excuse for claiming that she wasn't ready. Pandora was
rather hoping that he would be late so that she could
be magnanimous about not minding waiting, but she
had no such luck. The big car drew into the courtyard
on the stroke of eleven.

In spite of a weekend spent insisting to herself that
she didn't care in the least what he thought of her, Ran
had only to get out of the car for Pandora's heart to
lurch to her throat and stick there, hammering frantically. She fought it down as Ran shut the door and
turned to see her standing barefoot by the flowers in
the yellow dress, clutching the watering can with both

hands. Her skin was warm in the sunlight and the tumbling dark hair framed the pure lines of her face.

For a moment, he just stood there, looking at her. Pandora couldn't read his expression but for some reason she put down the watering can, very carefully. He was dressed casually in jeans and a dark green shirt, but nothing could disguise the power of the lean frame or the jolting impact of his presence, and when she looked into the grey eyes it was as if the earth had jarred to an abrupt halt, leaving her breathless and giddy.

Then Ran was walking across the courtyard towards her and time stumbled back into motion. In spite of the bright sunshine, Pandora felt oddly shaken, as if she had missed a step in the dark.

'Don't you ever wear shoes?' he asked by way of a greeting, looking down at her bare feet, his expression still unreadable.

'Not if I can help it.' Her voice would have sounded quite normal if it hadn't seemed to be coming from a long way away. 'My feet always feel constricted in shoes.'

'Are you planning to go out to lunch barefoot as well?'

'I wish I could.' Pandora picked up her shoes from the mounting block and sat down on it, bending her head to brush the dust from her feet so that her hair fell forward to hide her face. Slipping on one of the elegant pumps he had paid for, she glanced up at Ran. He was staring at her as if he had never seen her before, and she faltered with her hand still on the shoe. 'Is something the matter?'

'No.' His look was quickly shuttered. 'I was just thinking that you've gone to a lot of trouble to make yourself look nice for Quentin,' he said brusquely.

Pandora stood up and brushed off her dress as she wiggled her other foot into the second shoe. 'It was such an expensive dress it seems a shame not to wear it.'

'Especially when it had such an effect on Quentin last time?'

'You don't mind me wearing it, do you?' she said, suddenly uncertain. 'I suppose it is your dress.'

Ran looked sardonic. 'I can't see that I'm going to get much use out of it, can you?'

'You might like to take it back for Cindy.'

An odd expression flitted across face, almost as if he was trying to remember who Cindy was. 'It's not her style,' he said. 'I think you'd better keep it as a souvenir of me.'

A souvenir. Something to remember him by in years to come. Pandora tried to imagine pulling the dress out of a wardrobe one day and having a vague memory of a man with grey eyes and an inflexible mouth, but she couldn't do it. His image was so deeply seared onto her consciousness that she didn't think it would ever fade.

'Well. . .thank you. . .' She trailed off as he casually lifted her hair to run it through his fingers. He was so close that she could almost feel the hardness of his body. She could see him breathing, see the pulse beating in his throat. 'Wh-what are you doing?'

'Just checking for twigs.'

Was that a smile lurking around his mouth? Pandora felt her stomach disappear. She tried to say something light, but her jaw wouldn't work properly and she could only stand there in the sunlight with his hands in her hair and strum with awareness of him.

As he wound the soft hair around his fingers, his grip tightened almost imperceptibly. For one dazzling, heart-stopping moment Pandora was certain that he was going to kiss her, but instead he smoothed her hair reluctantly away from her face and withdrew his hands, letting one of them slide slowly down her cheek to her throat so that he could draw his thumb along her jawline in a feather-light caress.

'I see you brush your hair for Quentin,' was all he said, and the smile in his voice had gone, to be replaced by a faint edge of bleakness.

She could hardly tell him that the only person she had thought about when she'd got ready that morning had been him. Her face was burning, her jaw marked with a scorched, throbbing line which bore, she was sure, the imprint of every whorl on his thumb. Awash with a seething mixture of disappointment, relief and dark bewitchment, incapable of speaking, Pandora nodded dumbly and he stepped back abruptly.

'We'd better go.'

They hardly spoke in the car. Ran drove in preoccupied silence and Pandora stared out of the window at the lush summer verges and the green fields rolling up to the hills without seeing any of them. She kept her hands clutched tightly together in her lap to stop them creeping up to nurse her face, which still throbbed and tingled.

He's leaving soon, she reminded herself almost desperately. You'll probably never see him again after tomorrow. Hadn't Ran made it crystal-clear that as far as he was concerned the sooner their association came to an end the better? When the Americans had gone, they would go their separate ways, and he obviously couldn't wait.

'We can forget each other.' Wasn't that what he had said?

Pandora tried to imagine forgetting Ran, forgetting how she felt whenever he touched her, but it was like trying to think about the size of the universe—so impossible to comprehend that it made her feel dizzy and slightly sick. Everything was different now. It wasn't so much that she had changed. It was more as if she had put on a pair of glasses and was suddenly seeing things in a completely different way.

Ran hadn't changed either. He was arrogant and unfeeling and at times downright unpleasant, but Pandora knew instinctively that she would never be able to meet a man in the future without comparing him with the man sitting beside her now as the country-side slid noiselessly past the car. Would his eyes be as grey? His body as hard? His mouth as cool? Would the merest brush of his hand be as able to send a shiver of sensation down her spine?

Of course, Pandora told herself. There was absolutely no reason why she shouldn't meet a man who would wipe all thoughts of Ran and everyone else from her mind. What *would* he be like, though? It had been Ran who had asked her that. Was that why now, when she tried to picture her ideal man, it was Ran's face that shimmered just behind her eyelids? Pandora tried to banish it by conjuring up the faces of previous boyfriends, but they were all just a blur now. Not one of them stood out; there was not one whose touch she could recall the way she could remember Ran's, not one she had been in love with.

Pandora didn't quite know what being in love would be like, but she knew it wouldn't be the undemanding friendship and affection she had shared with past boyfriends, most of whom had drifted comfortably into the role of friends. Real love wouldn't be like that. It would be wonderful, glorious, uncompromising. Her heart would leap and her bones would melt. . .the way they did whenever she looked at Ran's mouth, an insidious inner voice added, and Pandora stiffened as she realised the treacherous way her thoughts were leading her.

There wasn't any point in even *thinking* about falling in love with Ran Masterson. Even if he hadn't had his perfect open relationship with perfect Cindy, there was no way he would ever be interested in her. She might as well fall in love with the stuffed bear in his hall.

Ran dropped her right outside the gallery. 'I'll meet you here at two o'clock,' he said briefly. Pandora stood on the pavement and watched him pull out into the traffic and wondered why she felt so forlorn. She was the one who had insisted on coming to lunch with Quentin, wasn't she? Why couldn't she remember why she had wanted to see him so much?

She *did* want to see him. Pandora turned and walked resolutely up the steps to the gallery. She had already decided that she wasn't going to do anything stupid like fall in love with Ran Masterson, so there wasn't any point in wishing that she were still sitting silently in the car beside him instead of going out to lunch with a charming, handsome man.

Quentin was flatteringly delighted to see her, but when he kissed her on both cheeks Pandora felt only the line of fire along her jaw where Ran's touch still burned. She smiled and chatted vivaciously all through lunch, and hoped that Quentin didn't realise how detached she felt. He was obviously exerting himself to be extra charming, yet Pandora hardly noticed. Why did nothing feel as real, as sharply focused as when Ran was there? And why did she keep glancing surreptitiously at her watch to see how long it was until two o'clock?

Lunch seemed to last for ever. When they got back to the gallery, Ran was already waiting outside, looking grim and dark and formidable. He glowered at Pandora when he saw her coming, and she immediately linked her arm through Quentin's and smiled charmingly up at him. How could she have wasted a delicious lunch thinking about a man who couldn't even be bothered to smile when he saw her?

'Are you ready?' he said to her, nodding curtly at Quentin.

'Almost.' Pandora turned to Quentin, who was looking a bit nonplussed by Ran's sudden appearance, and proceeded to thank him as if he had given her the lunch of a lifetime. Ran's basilisk's stare was all she had hoped for. 'Thank you again, Quentin,' she said, kissing him in what Ran would not doubt have called an 'arty' fashion. 'That was super. Let's do it again soon.'

'Do what again soon?' scowled Ran, bearing her off and leaving a delighted if puzzled Quentin behind them.

Pandora didn't know what was wrong with her. She had spent the entire lunch wishing that Ran were there, but no sooner had she laid eyes on him than she had started behaving as if she couldn't bear to be wrenched away from Quentin. Proof positive that she stood in no danger of falling in love with him, Pandora decided, and was comforted by the thought, though right now it was hard to believe that she had even considered the possibility. Ran strode along, black-browed, one hard hand at her elbow so that she had to trot to keep up with him.

Confused by the way her feelings towards him kept swinging from aggravation to dangerous attraction and back to acute dislike, Pandora took refuge in bad temper, and they were scratchy and snappy with each other as they went round the supermarket. Ran insisted on her handing over her shopping list and then was infuriated by it.

'Why couldn't you have put it in some kind of order?' he demanded, marching angrily back to the vegetable section when he discovered onions and tomatoes only by the time he had reached the baking shelves several aisles away.

Pandora snatched the list back out of his hand. 'Because *I* don't need to! We're not all so repressed we can't cope with a shopping list without analysing it.'

'There's nothing repressed about a bit of efficiency,' he snapped back. 'I'd have thought it would make all the difference to *your* life. You seem to exist in a constant state of muddle.'

'Well, I'd rather live with muddle than with a man who organises his shopping lists!'

'Believe me, I wouldn't want you!' snarled Ran, and they glared at each other.

They squabbled all the way home. Pandora was so cross by that stage that she didn't notice where Ran was going until the car swept up to the front door of Kendrick Hall and stopped with an angry spray of gravel.

'Am I supposed to walk home from here?'

'It wouldn't kill you,' he said with a nasty look. 'I'd have thought it was a sensible idea to unload the shopping here so that you don't have to bring it all down tomorrow, but if that's too *repressed* and *efficient* for you, then of course I'll drive you all the way back to the stables. We wouldn't want you to have to walk, would we? It would take all of. . .oh. . .a whole minute.'

Pandora got out and banged the door on his sarcasm. 'I suppose I may as well see the kitchen now I'm here,' she said ungraciously.

The hall was as gloomy and bizarre as she had

remembered. Pandora averted her eyes from the empty stand that had once held the Chinese vase and followed Ran down what seemed like an interminable corridor to a vast, old-fashioned kitchen, complete with an enormous table, an even bigger dresser and a panel of servants' bells. Two cast-iron ranges were set into the old fireplace. Pandora gazed at them in horror.

'I'm not going to have to cook in *those*, am I?'

For the first time, a gleam of amusement sprang into Ran's eyes. 'Fortunately for all of us, there's an electric cooker.' He pointed to where it stood, looking modern and out of place, next to an antiquated fridge. 'Apparently my uncle had a cook who insisted on a new cooker as one of her terms of employment.'

'I'm not surprised.' Pandora opened a drawer and wrinkled her nose at the array of implements. 'Have you ever thought of opening this place as a museum?'

'If you think this is bad, wait until you see the rest of the house,' said Ran, putting the last of the carrier bags on the table. 'Since you're here, I might as well show you round now. You might not have time tomorrow, and it wouldn't look very good if you got lost in what was supposed to be your own home.'

It wouldn't be that hard to do either, Pandora mused as he proceeded to give her a guided tour. There were so many steps and twisting staircases leading up to hidden rooms, and passages turning into yet more corridors, that Pandora began to feel quite giddy. As Ran had warned, the house had been virtually untouched since the beginning of the century, and although it had a dusty, quirky charm of its own it was obviously going to cost a fortune to modernise completely. Pandora thought of the Chinese vase and winced. It was the first time she had appreciated just what a financial burden Ran had inherited, and suddenly acting as his wife for a night didn't seem too high a price to pay for what Homer had done.

CHAPTER FIVE

CONSCIOUS of a twinge of guilt at the ungracious way she had behaved, Pandora glanced at Ran. He was pointing out some of the portraits that hung in gloomy array around the dining room, and a shaft of sunlight sliding through the dusty windows slanted across his face, highlighting the angle of his cheek and just catching the cool curve of his mouth.

Pandora wished she hadn't noticed. She stared fixedly at a portrait of one of Ran's dour Victorian ancestors but all she could see was a familiar line of cheek and jaw. Ran's voice seemed to reverberate down her spine and when he stepped towards her as he moved to the door she leapt away as if he had tipped a boiling pot into her path.

Ran raised an eyebrow but didn't comment. He continued with the tour of the house, in spite of the fact that Pandora's comments were increasingly distracted. It was so much easier when she could hate him. Now, for some reason, the antagonism had seeped out of the atmosphere to be replaced by a newer, more highly charged tension that left Pandora twanging with awareness. She couldn't look at Ran directly, and if he brushed against her in a doorway or put out his hand to warn her about an unexpected step she flinched.

'I hope you're going to do better than this tomorrow,' said Ran caustically as he pushed open the French windows which led out to the terrace from the drawing room.

'What do you mean?' Pandora edged cautiously past him without touching.

'I mean that you're carrying on like a frightened virgin instead of a loving wife. Myra and Elaine are hardly going to be impressed by the happiness of our marriage if they see you wincing and flinching every time I come near you.'

Faint colour seeped into her cheeks. 'How would you like me to carry on?' she asked defensively.

'All I want you to do is behave like a normal wife,' he said, with a gesture of impatience.

'I've never been married,' said Pandora. 'I don't *know* how a normal wife behaves.'

'Don't you?' Before she quite knew what was happening, she found herself pressed back against one of the worn stone lions that guarded the top of the terrace steps and staring up into Ran's angry face. His expression was that of a man goaded beyond endurance, but even as her eyes widened in alarm the anger faded and something quite different took its place, something that made the breath catch in Pandora's throat and slowed her heart until she was sure that it must stop altogether.

She felt as if she was teetering on the edge of a precipice, with only Ran's iron hands on her arms between her and a vertiginous fall. He held her pinned against the sun-warmed stone back of the lion, but as he looked down at her his hands slid up, with an agonising lack of haste, to encircle her throat and he pushed up her chin with his thumbs. 'Do you really not know how a real wife behaves, Pandora?' he asked softly.

'I. . .I. . .' Tangled up in a tightening knot of alarm and anticipation and a secret, shameful yearning,

Pandora could only stammer helplessly, and Ran's eyes blazed a sudden, brilliant grey as he bent his head.

'She behaves as if she'd be pleased if her husband did this,' he said, and then his mouth was on hers and the precipice slipped beneath Pandora's feet and she had to clutch at him to stop herself falling into an abyss of swirling, dangerous emotion. His kiss was fiercely demanding at first, the kiss of a man provoked into doing something he had just decided not to do. It was the kiss that was intended to teach Pandora a lesson, but somehow, somewhere along the line, intention went awry and suddenly they were kissing each other with a passion that caught them both unawares, dissolving the tension and the anger in a spinning sweetness.

Pandora succumbed to it with only a token murmur of protest and she loosened her clutch on his shirt to slide her arms up around Ran's neck as he gathered her closer. Leaning into the hard, reassuring strength of his body, she knew in some deep, instinctive part of her that she had been hungering for this moment ever since he had kissed her on the photographer's seat. She had wanted to know how his body would feel, and what it would be like to press into it, just as she was doing now. She had guessed that it would be like this—solid and unyielding—but how could she have known how exciting it would be to feel his arms tight around her, his hands sliding seductively down her spine?

With a muttered exclamation, Ran tangled his fingers in her hair and kissed his way tantalisingly along her jaw to her earlobe, and then slowly, deliberately down her throat. Pandora gasped at the piercing pleasure of his lips, so warm and sure against her skin. Her eyes were closed, her head tipped back as she arched towards him, intoxicated by the feel and the touch and the taste of him.

'Now you look more like a wife,' murmured Ran, beginning to retrace the searing path of his kisses.

His words filtered slowly through the enchanted haze and Pandora's eyes opened. Behind Ran's dark head, she could see the old stone walls of the house, and in an odd, irrelevant flash she noticed that they were exactly the same uncompromising grey as his eyes. At almost the same moment she realised what she was doing and she stiffened at the cold, swamping wave of reality.

Ran raised his head as he felt her reaction and his eyes were dark and unreadable. 'You see,' he said. 'You *do* know how to behave like a wife.'

Pandora's face flooded with colour and she wrenched herself out of his arms. Her legs were shaking and her eyes were huge and dark. She swallowed, opened her mouth to say something dignified, but nothing came out.

'You shouldn't have any problem convincing Elaine and Myra if you look like that tomorrow,' Ran went on in the same tone of mock approval, and casually tucked a strand of her wildly dishevelled hair behind her ear.

Pandora jerked her head away. 'I hope I'll be able to convince them without that sort of assistance,' she managed unsteadily.

'At least you've demonstrated that you can do it when you try,' he said. 'I was beginning to wonder.'

A demonstration? Was that all that bewitching kiss had been for him? How could he stand there looking so cool and restrained and so utterly unmoved when her body was still booming and strumming with reaction? Pandora didn't know whether she wanted to hit him or to cast herself back into his arms and beg him to tell her that he had felt that sweetness too.

In the end she did neither. Instead, she took a step

back and steadied her voice with an enormous effort. 'I'm a better actress than you think,' she said.

His eyes narrowed slightly. 'Are you now?' he said. 'Do you act as well with Quentin?'

'I don't need to act with Quentin,' she said, meeting his eyes directly, and his face closed.

'Well, just make sure you act tomorrow,' he said harshly. 'And don't forget that your performance had better be worth thirty thousand pounds!'

'I'm hardly likely to forget,' said Pandora, walking towards the steps on legs that felt like cotton wool. 'Do you think I'd have kissed you at all if it wasn't for that thirty thousand pounds. . .?' To her horror, her attempt to sound contemptuous trailed off into a dangerous wobble, and, terrified in case she broke down in front of him, she turned and ran down the steps and across the lawn towards the stables before Ran could reply.

Her first action on reaching the safety of home was to take the yellow roses which were still looking gorgeous in the sitting room and dump them in the bin. Her second was to sit down at the kitchen table and have a good cry.

How could he have kissed her like that and not meant it? How could she have kissed him back as if she had? The feel of him was still rippling over her skin, vibrating through her. She could still feel the powerful shoulders beneath her hands and the nerves in her throat jumped and tingled as if his lips were still pressed there, sending the same thrill shivering down her spine.

Pandora squeezed her eyes closed to shut out the image of the way she had arched against him, but it didn't do any good. She drew in a deep, steadying breath. She had to stop this. Tomorrow she had to face Ran again, and there was no way she was going to let him know that he had reduced her to tears!

Jumping to her feet, she washed her tear-stained face in cold water and felt better. All she had to do was get through tomorrow. She would play her part as she had promised, but behind the scenes she would make it absolutely clear to Ran Masterson that she couldn't wait for it all to be over. She would be poised. She would be coolly unconcerned. She wouldn't even *think* about how he had kissed her.

Well, she would try not to. . .

The next morning she packed an overnight bag, collected Homer's bowl and put him on the lead. Then she walked calmly down to Kendrick Hall and rang the doorbell. She could hear it clanging away in the distance.

'Ah, there you are,' said Ran when he opened the door, quite as if he had last seen her ten minutes ago in the most innocuous of circumstances, instead of fleeing across the grass after a shattering kiss.

'Good morning.' That was just the right tone, Pandora thought, pleased: politeness with a chilly edge.

Ran didn't appear to notice her frigid new image. His eyes had fallen on Homer, who was wagging his tail eagerly by her side. 'You're not planning on bringing that dog in with you, are you?'

'Yes, I am. I can't leave him for all that time, so you'll just have to put up with him. He'll just settle down somewhere.'

'Well, if he breaks anything else, he'll be as stuffed as that bear,' Ran warned, standing back to let them in.

In spite of her confident air, Pandora was glad that she had Homer on the lead. He growled at the bear, but allowed himself to be dragged past to the kitchen and shut in. Things were going well so far, Pandora thought. She had worried about what to do with Homer, but as long as he stayed in the kitchen he shouldn't be too much trouble. As for herself, she was rather pleased with her cool composure. It was just a pity that Ran didn't seem to be noticeably daunted.

'Where shall I put my things?' she asked, gesturing at her bag. 'I'd like to hang up my dress.'

'I'll take you up to my room,' said Ran, and her careful poise slipped slightly at the prospect of the night to come.

Don't even think about it, she told herself as she followed Ran up the grand staircase to a wide landing.

'These are the best spare rooms,' Ran said, opening the doors into two large, sunny rooms with faded wallpaper and heavy, old-fashioned furniture. 'I thought we'd put Myra and Elaine in one each. There's a bathroom just there.' He pointed across the landing before turning to open a third door. 'This is my room. The bedrooms are all so close together that it would be very obvious if we weren't sharing one.'

'I suppose so.' Pandora stepped inside his room almost grudgingly. Ran hadn't done anything to make the room his own. It might as well have been a hotel room, albeit a spartan one. There were no photographs on the chest of drawers, no pictures on the walls. It was as if he was just passing through.

As he was.

Her eyes moved slowly around the room as she tried to avoid looking at the enormous wooden bed. It was impossible not to think of Ran lying there, turning in sleep to fling an arm across the white sheet.

She cleared her throat. She was cool and composed, wasn't she? A little thing like imagining Ran in bed wasn't going to bother her. 'Is there somewhere for me to sleep tonight?' she asked, carefully casual.

'What's wrong with the bed?'

'Won't you be sleeping in it?'

'Look at the size of it, Pandora!' said Ran impatiently. 'You could sleep four in it comfortably. It ought to be more than big enough for both of us.'

'I am not sleeping in a bed with you!' Pandora's voice rose in spite of herself.

Ran looked testy. 'What else do you suggest?'

'You could sleep on the sofa,' she said, indicating a chesterfield that had seen much better days. The worn red leather was cracked and lumpy and it looked extremely uncomfortable, but it would be better than the floor.

'I could,' Ran agreed. 'But I fail to see why I should spend an uncomfortable night on that thing when there's a perfectly good bed available. You sleep on it if it bothers you so much.'

'I shall,' said Pandora defiantly. There was no way she was going to climb into bed with Ran! She might be composed but she wasn't *that* composed.

Dropping her bag onto the chesterfield, she pulled out the grey evening dress her mother had once given her and shook it out. 'Have you got a hanger?'

Ran pulled one out of the mahogany wardrobe and tossed it across to her, watching moodily as she hung the dress up on the door. 'Where's the yellow dress?' he asked. 'I hope you're not planning to greet Myra and Elaine in that old thing you've got on now?'

'This "old thing", as you call it, is my favourite dress,' said Pandora coldly, hoping he wouldn't pursue the subject of the yellow outfit. The once bright greens and blues were faded now, but that was only to be expected after a few years, and the material was soft and as comfortable as an old friend.

'No doubt it's suitable for cooking and cleaning, but

you can't be wearing it when they arrive,' said Ran.
'Why didn't you bring the yellow dress with you to
change into later?'

Faint colour stained Pandora's cheeks and she busied
herself twitching out the folds of the grey dress. 'It's
stained. I'll have to take it to the cleaners.'

'Stained? How? Did you drop something down it?'

'No, I did not!' she snapped, provoked out of her
calm at last. 'If you must know, it was badly stained by
moss, and if I could have done anything about it,
believe me, I would have done!' She hadn't discovered
the stain until she had taken off the dress last night and
the sight of it had brought back the whole scene on the
terrace just when she had succeeded in calming herself
down.

Ran didn't seem to have registered the significance
of her reference to moss. 'Damn! I wanted you to be
wearing that when they arrived.'

'You should have thought of that before you went
around pressing me up against stone lions!' said
Pandora tartly before she could stop herself.

Realisation gleamed in the grey eyes. 'Ah...when
you were practising your acting technique?'

'That's one way of putting it, yes,' she said stiffly.

He tutted. 'I would have thought that an experienced
actress like you would have taken better care of her
costume!'

Pandora cast him a look of dislike. 'Hadn't we better
get on?'

'Yes.' Ran was instantly brisk. 'You'd better do their
rooms first, then you can make the rooms downstairs
look suitably welcoming, and after that you might as
well get on with the cooking.'

'I thought you wanted me to act as a wife, not a
slave,' she muttered sourly.

He held open the door with mock courtesy. 'Think yourself lucky it's only a temporary arrangement! Oh, and that reminds me. . .' Reaching into the pocket of his blue shirt, he pulled out a couple of rings. 'You'd better see if these fit.'

'What for?'

'Don't be dense, Pandora. The Americans are bound to notice if you're not wearing a wedding ring. I didn't even think about it for the photographs, but fortunately your hands don't show in the one I've chosen.'

Pandora stared at him. 'You've *bought* me rings just for one night?'

'Of course I haven't,' he said irritably. 'I found them in a jewellery box in the study.'

'But whose are they?' She looked at the rings in his hand as if they might bite.

'They seem to have been my grandmother's, which presumably makes them mine now.'

Pandora looked dubious. 'I don't really like the idea of wearing someone else's rings.'

'Do you like the idea of repaying thirty thousand pounds any better?' said Ran in a deceptively pleasant voice, and, recognising the steel that lay behind his tone, she gave up and held out her left hand reluctantly.

He took it and slid a magnificent sapphire and diamond ring onto her third finger, and then a plain gold band. Pandora watched his strong brown fingers holding her own and something twisted inside her so sharply that she caught her breath, and Ran glanced at her face.

She coloured beneath that acute grey gaze. 'They're beautiful,' she said with difficulty.

Ran didn't release her hand immediately, but rubbed his thumb absently over the sparkling stones. 'Lucky they fit.'

Pandora had wild thoughts of Cinderella and how disappointed she would have been if Prince Charming had reacted in that dispassionate tone when he'd discovered that the glass slipper fitted. She was acutely conscious of his fingers touching hers, warm and strong and steady.

'You should have kept them until you found a girl you really wanted to give them to,' she said unevenly.

'Perhaps,' he said. 'But in the meantime you're all I've got.'

Slowly, unwillingly, Pandora lifted her eyes from their linked hands to look up at him, and her heart began to thud and thump, booming in her ears and echoing along her veins. The memory of yesterday's kiss strummed between them like a tangible thing. Ran was thinking of it too, she knew. Was he remembering his hands in her hair, his lips at her throat, her body soft and yielding in his arms?

'Just for tonight,' she said in a voice that belonged to someone else, and Ran's eyes shuttered as he dropped her hand.

'Just for tonight,' he agreed.

The rings felt heavy and awkward on Pandora's hands as she made up the beds in the spare rooms. The diamonds kept glinting in the sunlight, catching distractingly at the edge of her vision. Ran had produced some sheets and brusquely announced that he would leave her to it. Pandora knew that she ought to resent him, but, if anything, she was grateful for something to do. It stopped her thinking too much about that timeless moment in the doorway when he had put the rings on her finger, or allowing her mind to drift into the dangerous channels of wondering what it would feel like to be wearing those rings in other circumstances—

because Ran wanted her to wear them for ever and not just for a night.

Pandora straightened the cover on the bed and stood back. The sooner she found another job to occupy her mind the better. She ran her finger along the mantel-piece, but it wasn't dusty. Ran had either cleaned the rooms himself or got someone else to clean them, but the house still felt blank and unwelcoming. It needed life more than cleaning. It needed a family—children to shout and laugh and argue. It needed love.

The one thing Ran wouldn't give.

If she couldn't provide a family, she could at least provide flowers, Pandora decided philosophically. She found a pair of secateurs in the scullery and wandered out into the garden, taking Homer with her for company. There was no sign of Ran. Outside, the air was soft and sweet and bees drowsed over the overgrown borders.

The garden had been sadly neglected for some time and everything had grown wild, but she found pale blue campanulas and creamy meadowsweet, leggy daisies and deep blue spires of salvia, sweet williams and white delphiniums and, tumbling over the wall of the kitchen garden, a glorious display of pink roses with fragrant, velvety petals.

Ran was crossing the hall to his study when Pandora came in through the front door, her arms full of flowers and the absurd-looking dog at her heels. In the soft, faded dress she seemed to bring with her the warmth and fragrance of the summer garden, dissipating the gloom of the hall.

She stopped dead when she saw him, and the tranquillity which had enveloped her as she'd gathered the flowers fizzled abruptly away. As they looked at each other wordlessly across the hall, even the ticking of the

grandfather clock under the stairs seemed to stop, then
it whirred itself suddenly back into life and struck the
hour with such a loud 'bong' that Ran and Pandora
jumped as if a gun had gone off. Without thinking, they
smiled at each other, and for one glorious moment they
were just a man and a girl, alone with a dog and a
stuffed bear and the motes of dust hanging motionless
in the sunbeams that poured through the open door.

The moment lasted as long as it took the clock to
strike twelve sonorous times, but with the last stroke
the magic vanished. Reality came crowding back with
all its tension and memories. The vase, the debt,
yesterday's kiss. Cindy and the inevitability of Ran's
departure. For a space there, Pandora had forgotten
them all, but she remembered them now, and her smile
faded at the same time as Ran's.

She looked down at the flowers, unable to meet his
eyes. 'I. . .er. . . I'd better get on.'

'Yes.' Ran sounded oddly uncertain. He looked as if
he wanted to say something else but in the end he just
said yes again and disappeared abruptly into his study.

Pandora stood looking at the door as it shut behind
him. Inexplicable tears stung her eyes and she blinked
them furiously away. What was there to cry about?
Ran had smiled and then shut himself in his study.
There was nothing there to account for this sudden
feeling of desolation, as if she had held something
precious in her hands, only to let it slip through her
fingers.

Telling herself not to be so stupid, Pandora carried
the flowers through to the pantry and searched through
the cupboards for some vases. By the time she had
filled them with haphazard arrangements of flowers she
had even managed to persuade herself that nothing had
happened.

Nothing *had* happened. She had come through the door and seen Ran and the clock had struck and then they had smiled at each other, and he had gone into his study and shut the door. Hardly the ingredients of a melodrama!

The flowers transformed the bedrooms. Pandora had so many left over that she was able to stand some delphiniums on a chest on the landing, fill bowls for the drawing room and dining room and still have some sweet williams to spare. She considered putting them in the hall but decided that there was no point in even trying to compete with a bear and a stuffed python. It was a shame to waste them, though.

Pandora stood on the landing, holding the vase uncertainly between her hands, then, on an impulse, took them into Ran's room and set them down on the chest of drawers. There. That would show that she wasn't in the least bit nervous about sharing a room with him.

She was polishing the dining-room table about an hour later when Ran came out of the study at last. He paused in the doorway when he saw her.

'How are you getting on?' His voice was cool, his expression guarded. It was hard to believe that this was the same man who had smiled at her across the hall.

'All right.' Pandora straightened from the table. She was hot and flushed from the vigorous polishing, and she wiped her cheeks with the back of her arm. 'I'm going to get the meal ready as soon as I've finished here.'

'Good.' Ran hesitated. 'I'm going to see if I can find some wine in the cellar. If not, I'll have to go out and get some.'

'Fine.' How could they be this stilted with each other when they had argued as if they had known each other for years? When they had kissed as if they were lovers? The cloth forgotten in her hand, Pandora watched him open a door and disappear down some steps. It was all very well deciding to be cool and polite, she mused, but it was much less awkward when they were fighting.

Or kissing. The awkwardness only came afterwards.

With a tiny sigh, Pandora reapplied herself to her polishing. When the phone rang in the study next door a couple of minutes later, she ignored it at first, thinking that Ran would answer it, but he obviously couldn't hear the telephone down in the cellar. The study was the one room Ran hadn't shown her and Pandora opened the door with a sense of intrusion. Lined with bookcases, it was a large, high-ceilinged room, with a comfortably shabby air. The phone stood on a wide desk which was piled high with buff files and account books.

Pandora picked it up cautiously. 'Hello?'

'Hi.' The warm, confident American voice at the other end sounded surprised. 'Is Ran there, please?'

'Who's calling?' said Pandora coldly, even though she knew at once who it must be.

'It's Cindy.'

Pandora wanted to tell her that he wasn't there and put the phone down, but instead she grudgingly said that she would get him for her.

'Cindy's on the phone,' she shouted down the cellar steps.

There was a momentary hesitation. 'Can you tell her that I'm just coming?'

So now she was a secretary as well as a maid of all work! Refusing to analyse why she felt so cross, Pandora grumbled her way back to the phone. 'He's just coming,' she said curtly, but she hardly needed to have bothered. Ran was already there, holding out his hand for the receiver.

'Hello, Cindy,' Pandora heard him say as she went out. 'What?' He hesitated. 'Oh. . .that was just the housekeeper.'

'Just the housekeeper' indeed! Pandora took great pleasure in slamming the study door shut behind her and stalked off to the kitchen, where she spent the next two hours banging around the pots and pans in an effort to work off her temper. It was not the best frame of mind in which to tackle the cooking for a dinner party. After leafing through all Celia's cookery books, she had finally decided to try making smoked-trout mousse and chicken with an interesting-sounding sauce, and her mother had given her what she she'd promised faithfully was a foolproof recipe for lemon tart.

It might have been foolproof, but it wasn't nearly as simple as her mother had made it sound, and the mousse and the chicken, neither of which had looked too complicated when she had read through the recipes, both turned out to be fiendishly complex in practice. In the end, Pandora gave up the recipes and opted for guessing wildly instead, too cross to care what the meal tasted like anyway. What did a housekeeper care about the dinner? She was just a *servant*.

Pandora picked up the packet of ready-made pastry she had insisted on buying in spite of Ran's mutterings about wanting everything to be home-made. 'You make it if you're so concerned about it,' she had said. 'I'll never be able to make pastry that's as good as this, and I'm not even going to try. I'm not going to attempt any baking either, so we may as well buy a cake or some scones and lie.'

Now she scowled at the instructions on the back of the packet. Had Cindy rung off yet, or was Ran still whispering sweet nothings down the phone? Was he telling her what a treasure his new housekeeper was, or were they laughing together about how ruthlessly he was exploiting the girl next door? Or, worse, were they ignoring her completely and talking about how soon they would be together again?

Preoccupied with her own thoughts, Pandora completely failed to realise that she had left the door open, or to wonder where Homer was. She found out when Ran hauled him into the kitchen just after three o'clock.

'There's not much point in making the guest rooms look nice if you're going to encourage your dog to roll on the beds!' he said, looking as bad-tempered as Pandora felt.

'I might have known it would be my fault!' she snapped, shaking flour indiscriminately over the kitchen table. 'In case you haven't noticed, I've been slaving for you all day. I haven't had time to encourage Homer to do anything!'

'He obviously hasn't had any discouragement from getting on beds before,' said Ran, glowering down at Homer, who only lolled his tongue out happily in return, quite unchastened. 'I found him looking quite at home with his head on the pillow. Clearly he doesn't share your hang-ups about strange beds!'

'He doesn't share my hang-ups about strange men either!' Pandora retorted waspishly. 'If you're so anxious for a companion tonight, ask Homer. I'm sure he'd be happy to share his bed with you—he's very undiscriminating!'

'I'm not *anxious* for you to sleep with me,' Ran said, thin-lipped. 'I merely think you're behaving stupidly about the whole idea. It may not be a normal situation but surely two rational adults ought to be able to spend a night together without carrying on like something out of a Victorian melodrama?'

'I am *not* carrying on!' Pandora banged down the sieve and stalked over to the dresser to consult her recipe again. 'You're the one in the bad mood! What's the matter? Didn't Cindy like the fact that you had a *housekeeper*? I thought the whole point about open relationships was that you didn't lie to each other!'

Ran looked thunderous. 'You're a fine one to talk about lying!'

'*Me?*' she exclaimed in outraged astonishment, slamming the recipe book shut and turning from the dresser. 'I haven't been telling my girlfriend that the young woman obviously alone in the house with me is just a servant!'

'No, but you lied yesterday, didn't you?'

'When?' she asked furiously.

'When you said you were just acting when I kissed you.' Ran caught her arm, swinging her away from the dresser and back against the wall beneath the array of servants' bells. 'No one could act as well as that.'

Pandora tried to pull her arm free of his iron grip, but it was useless. 'I told you I was a better actress than you thought,' she said, but her eyes were wary.

'You're not that good, Pandora.' His eyes were bright with anger and something else, his fingers digging into her bare arm. 'Or do you kiss everyone like that? Are you as warm and yielding when Quentin takes you in his arms?'

'It's different when the man you love kisses you,' said Pandora, trembling but still defiant.

Ran's eyes gleamed suddenly. 'Is it now? What's it like when Quentin kisses you, Pandora?' He took her jaw in his free hand to tilt her head back against the wall. 'Is it like this?'

Pandora opened her mouth to reply, but it was too late. She never even knew whether she had been going to say yes or no as his lips came down on hers and the tension that had been building between them all day exploded into a wild, whirling excitement. At the last moment, she rammed her hands against his chest in a futile attempt to push away the lean, taut body pressing her inexorably into the wall, but he was too strong, too solid, and as she spun helplessly before the rush of sensation she found herself clinging to him as her one anchor to reality.

His lips were hard and angry at first, and Pandora fought desperately to resist the electrifying feelings that surged through her, but it was as if the kiss had acquired a power of its own that was stronger than either of them. Imperceptibly, it changed and deepened, swirling them out into uncharted waters where the anger and the strain were submerged beneath a wave of desire and where Pandora forgot to fight any more.

Almost of their own accord, her hands crept down from their defensive position at his chest to encircle his waist and pull him back against the wall with her. She was dizzy with the feel of his body pressing into hers, hungry for the taste of his mouth and the touch of his lips searing kisses against her throat.

Ran sensed the change at once, and the hand at Pandora's jaw slid round to support the nape of her neck while the other drifted possessively down over the soft curves of her body to slip beneath her dress and explore the smooth length of her thigh with insistent demand, lifting her up to him until she arched her back and gasped with pleasure.

And then the bell went.

CHAPTER SIX

THE deafening jangle right over their heads worked as effectively as a bucket of water. Ran dropped Pandora back to earth, literally, as Homer went into a frenzy of barking and rushed to the front door.

'Saved by the bell,' he said a little unevenly. 'That must be Myra and Elaine.'

Pandora smoothed down her skirt with shaking hands, her eyes bright with a mixture of seething fury and excitement. 'Hadn't you better go and let them in?' she asked tightly.

'We'll go together.' It hadn't taken Ran any time to get his ragged breathing under control, she noticed resentfully, still struggling with her own. He reached out and brushed some flour out of her hair. 'Couldn't you have tidied yourself up a bit?'

'I haven't had *time* to tidy myself,' said Pandora, jerking away from his touch and glaring at him as she brushed herself down ineffectively. 'You can't have a cook, a housekeeper *and* an elegant wife.'

Ran surveyed her critically. No one would have guessed that only a few moments ago he had been sliding up her dress, holding her hard against him, kissing her. 'You still look a bit dishevelled.'

'Whose fault is that?' she snapped. She tried to smooth her hair, but her hands were shaking so much that she only succeeded in making matters worse.

Above their heads the bell clanged again and Ran glanced up. 'You'll just have to do,' he said. 'We'd better go. Are you ready?'

Ready? How could she be ready when her lips were still throbbing, her body still clamouring with shameful excitement and dark, swirling desire?

'Perfectly,' she lied.

Ran hadn't warned her how comically different Myra and Elaine looked. Elaine was tall and thin with short, straight hair, Myra small and round and curly, but they were both dressed with ferocious smartness and shared a vigour and dynamism that was initially overwhelming. Even without the shattering effect of Ran's kiss to contend with, Pandora would have felt limp in comparison as they surged into the hall, apologising effusively for being so early and eyeing Pandora with undisguised interest. These were obviously two very sharp ladies, and Pandora began to shuffle backwards, certain that she wouldn't fool them for a minute.

Ran saw her out of the corner of his eye and took a firm grip on her wrist, drawing her inexorably forward. 'This is my wife, Pandora.'

'Oh, you're just as gorgeous as Ran told us you were!' exclaimed Myra. 'We're so delighted we had the chance to meet you after all.'

Pandora thought it extremely unlikely that Ran had described her as gorgeous, but they were all waiting for her to say something. 'I'm sorry I wasn't here when you came before,' she said, and Ran, obviously relieved that she was going to play her part properly, released her wrist.

'We quite understand,' said Elaine comfortably. 'How *is* your mother?'

'She's fine,' said Pandora, surprised.

'Considering her recent operation,' Ran added quickly. 'I told Myra and Elaine how anxious you were to see your mother again when we came back from Mandibia, which is why you weren't here before.'

It was a pity he hadn't told *her* that. Pandora slid him a vengeful look, but managed a pretty smile for the Americans. 'She's much better.'

'That *is* good news,' said Myra. 'You must have been longing to come up here and see your new home. Is it what you expected?'

Pandora looked at the stuffed snake. 'Well, not quite.'

'What about some tea?' said Ran, ushering them all into the drawing room.

'That would be lovely, but we know we're earlier than we said we would be, so if you two were in the middle of anything do please carry on.'

If only they knew just what they had been doing! Pandora was unable to resist glancing at Ran. The cool grey eyes glimmered with amusement as they met hers, and she knew that he too was picturing them calmly continuing that angry, exciting kiss. It had been quite unforgivable of Ran to kiss her like that and she hated him for it, but still Pandora felt an insane bubble of laughter rising inside her, and she had to press her lips firmly together to stop herself grinning at him.

'We weren't doing anything in the least bit important,' she said to Myra and Elaine, but the challenging look was for Ran alone.

He met it blandly. 'Why don't I get the tea while you show Myra and Elaine to their rooms, *darling*?' he said, with just the faintest sarcastic edge to the endearment.

The American women didn't seem to notice. They followed Pandora up the carved wooden staircase, exclaiming at everything. 'We only had time for a quick look round before,' Myra confided. 'We're really looking forward to exploring the house properly. It looks so fascinating!'

'I don't know the way round very well myself yet,'

said Pandora with perfect honesty. 'But I'm sure Ran would be delighted to show you round again.' They were his guests, after all. Let *him* entertain them! 'You must ask him.'

'Ran is *such* a charming man!' sighed Elaine.

Only to some, Pandora thought sourly. He never bothered being charming to *her*. Her mind veered treacherously to the way he had stood in the courtyard yesterday and let his finger drift along her cheek, to how he had looked as he'd smiled at her across the hall, before she dismissed the images. Those didn't count. Most of the time he was infuriating and obnoxious and most definitely *not* charming.

'And he's obviously so in love with you,' Myra was adding enviously.

Pandora stumbled on the stairs and had to clutch at the banister to stop herself falling. 'I'm sorry?' She stared, quite forgetting that a wife might reasonably expect her husband to be in love with her.

Fortunately Myra was following behind and Elaine was occupied with helping her regain her balance and didn't notice Pandora's face. 'Oh, yes,' said Myra. 'We could tell by the way he talked about you, couldn't we, Elaine?'

Elaine nodded vigorously. 'Of course, he's so reserved and British, but he described you so exactly, we knew at once.'

'Really?' said Pandora politely, unable to think of anything else to say.

'And now that we've seen you together it's obvious that you're a perfect match.'

The Americans clearly weren't as sharp as they seemed, Pandora thought with relief, but they were so friendly that she was beginning to feel a little uncomfortable about deceiving them like this. She opened the door of the first bedroom. 'We've put one of you in here and one just across the landing,' she said a little desperately, hoping to change the subject, but they weren't easily diverted.

'How did you two meet?' Elaine asked once they had pronounced the rooms 'just perfect'.

Pandora's mind went blank. 'Ran and I?' she said, playing for time while she tried frantically to remember what story they had agreed on. It was something to do with Harry... 'Mandibia!' she gasped thankfully as memory clicked at last. 'We met in Africa,' she amended more calmly, conscious of the other women's curious looks. 'My brother was working out there, and I went out to visit him and met Ran.'

'And was it love at first sight?' asked Elaine coyly.

Pandora had a fleeting picture of Ran as she had first seen him, looking dark and formidable and very, very angry, and without warning something turned over inside her, leaving her jarred and breathless.

'No,' she said firmly, almost as if she was trying to convince herself. Not that she needed convincing, of course. 'Ran wasn't at all impressed by me. He thought I was very silly and I thought *he* was dour and disagreeable,' she added with feeling.

Myra laughed. 'It sounds like love at first sight to me!' she said inexplicably. 'It obviously didn't take long for you to change your minds, anyway! Didn't you get married out there?'

Had Ran said anything about where they had supposedly married? Pandora couldn't remember. 'We just went off and got married one day,' she said, deciding not to risk answering directly. 'Just the two of us.'

'How brave of you!' Elaine said admiringly. 'Of course, I suppose it was easier being away from your family in Africa, but still. . .Ran must have swept you off your feet! How did he propose to you?'

So much for them not asking any questions! Pandora was beginning to feel hunted. 'It was very romantic,' she prevaricated.

'Oh, it must have been! Alone together in the middle of Africa. . .I can just imagine it!'

It was more than Pandora could do. Her image of Africa was hazy, to say the least, but she had seen *Out of Africa* years ago and she would just have to draw on that. 'Yes, it was wonderful,' she said, heaving what she hoped sounded like a reminiscent sigh. 'Ran took me out on safari, and we sat under the stars. He'd been to so much trouble to make it special for me,' she went on, gaining confidence. In for a penny, in for a pound! 'We had a cloth for the table and silver and crystal glasses, and romantic music playing in the background.' The thought of Ran carefully transporting crystal glasses through the African bush was so incongruous that Pandora had to bite back another smile.

Myra and Elaine were both looking misty-eyed. 'It sounds just like *Out of Africa*!' sighed Myra.

'I'll go and see how Ran's getting on with the tea,' said Pandora hastily. 'Just come down when you're ready.'

She hurried down to the kitchen, where she found Ran heating up the scones. 'I thought you said they wouldn't ask any questions!' she said accusingly, flopping down into a chair and carefully avoiding looking at the wall where he had kissed her such a short time ago. 'I've just been interrogated about how we met.'

'I hope you remembered the story we agreed on?' said Ran, dourly spooning jam into a dish.

'Eventually. They wanted to know if we fell in love

at first sight, but I said you thought I was too silly for words.'

'How perspicacious of you!'

'But you obviously changed your mind,' said Pandora with an innocent look. 'You took me out on safari to propose, and arranged for a candlelit dinner under the stars, complete with silver and crystal glasses.'

'I did *what*?'

'And romantic music in the background,' she added, not displeased at the chance to pay him back just a little bit for that devastating kiss. 'I thought I'd better tell you in case they ask you how you managed to keep the champagne cool.'

'Champagne?' echoed Ran incredulously, clattering plates onto the tray. 'If I'd taken you to the bush, you'd have sat on a log and had tea in an enamel mug!'

'Yes, but I thought it might help your image if Myra and Elaine thought you had the sort of style that would impress your guests.'

'There's nothing wrong with my image,' he snapped. 'And if there was it wouldn't be helped by that kind of story. What on earth possessed you to tell them something as ridiculous as that?'

'You said I should make it up if they asked me something I didn't know,' Pandora protested, dipping her finger in the jam.

Ran smacked her hand aside. 'I meant make up something sensible, not indulge in some flight of fancy that any idiot could see wasn't true! What are Myra and Elaine going to think?'

'They think you're a real romantic underneath that reserved British exterior.' She nursed her sore hand with a resentful look. 'I can't think why they believed me. It must be obvious that you've never had a romantic thought in your life!'

'It's probably easier than thinking I've married a pathological liar,' he retorted, striding across the kitchen to slam down the switch of the kettle. 'What else am I supposed to have done, apart from make a complete fool of myself traipsing around the bush with a dinner service? You didn't have me wrestling with elephants or single-handedly rescuing you from marauding lions, did you?'

'No,' said Pandora, stung at his dismissal of her story. She didn't think it was that bad, given that she had had to make it up on the spur of the moment. 'We just made mad, passionate love under the stars, and afterwards you said you'd never let me go!'

Her tone was sarcastic, but she regretted the words as soon as they were out of her mouth. Ran glanced at the wall by the dresser where he had kissed her and then at Pandora, who was sitting at the table looking ruffled and suddenly unsure.

'Did I?' he said with heavy irony. 'I must have drunk too much of that champagne!'

Why had she had to mention making love? Pandora had followed the direction of his gaze, half expecting to see the scorched outline of her body where he had pressed her against the wall, and colour crept up into her cheeks as her blood pounded anew at the memory. If it was like that when Ran kissed her angrily, what would it be like if he really did make love to her under the stars?

Cindy could probably tell her, Pandora reminded herself bleakly. She watched Ran's back as he made the tea. 'Myra and Elaine thought it was a very touching story,' she said defiantly.

'Well, please keep any future stories a little less touching and a little more realistic!'

Ran carried the tea-tray through to the drawing

room, and Pandora followed with a plate of the scones that she had bought the day before, unblushingly accepting the credit for making them when Elaine commented on how delicious they were.

'You're obviously a good cook, Pandora.'

Pandora thought sinkingly of the dinner to come. 'Not really,' she said. 'My mother taught me how to make scones, but I'm afraid I'm still a bit of a beginner in the kitchen. Of course, I'm going to do a cookery course before our first guests arrive,' she added, struck by a moment of inspiration.

Myra nodded approvingly. 'It's good to see that you're committed to the idea,' she said, and Ran looked positively encouraging. 'I must say, it's noticeable how different the house feels already with a woman's touch. Elaine and I were just commenting on the flowers. They're charming!'

'I suppose you're planning some changes to the house, Pandora?' said Elaine. 'Have you decided on a decorative theme yet?'

'Pandora isn't organised enough to think in terms of decorative themes,' said Ran in a dry voice, and Pandora threw him a look before turning back to Elaine with a determinedly bright smile.

'Actually, I've got plenty of ideas.'

'You haven't said anything about this to me,' said Ran, pretending suspicion.

'I haven't had time,' said Pandora with a quelling look. It was bad enough having to convince Myra and Elaine without him putting her on the spot as well! She leant confidentially across to Myra. 'You know, we've hardly spent a moment together since we arrived.'

Myra looked understanding. 'There's always so much to do when you move into a new house, isn't there?'

'I certainly seem to be busy all day.' Pandora heaved

a martyred sigh and risked a glance at Ran, who looked
as if he couldn't quite decide whether to be amused or
irritated.

'Tell us how you see Kendrick Hall in the future,
Pandora,' he said with a faint edge of irony, and the
American women nodded their interest at his
suggestion.

'Well. . .' Put on the spot, Pandora floundered. 'I
don't like houses too formal,' she prevaricated. 'They
should be homes rather than decorative schemes,
places where children can run around and not worry
about whether the cushions are out of place.' The violet
eyes held a challenging sparkle as they met Ran's
warning stare. 'Or whether the dog is going to bump
into the furniture and smash some priceless heirloom.'

'Oh, I do so agree,' said Elaine. 'Houses should be
homes, not museums. Some of the places we visit are
beautiful, but somehow cold. Our clients prefer more
of a family atmosphere, which is why we liked Kendrick
Hall so much. I hope you won't think me rude if I say
we liked its eccentricity. We felt it had a lot of
potential.' She turned to Ran. 'I guess that's one of the
reasons we were so relieved to hear that you were
married after all. I know you're planning to do lots of
restoration work, but what this house needs more than
anything is someone to bring it to life. It must feel a
much warmer place already now that Pandora's here
with you.'

Ran glanced across at Pandora, who had just
dropped jam onto her dress and was rubbing at the
stain while the scone she held in her other hand
showered crumbs into her lap. She had missed the last
part of the conversation, but she looked up just then
and saw him watching her. There was an odd
expression in his eyes. Thinking that he had noticed

her making a mess again, she blushed faintly and put her scone back on her plate.

Ran looked back at Elaine. 'Yes,' he said slowly, sounding almost puzzled. 'It does.'

'It will be a wonderful place to bring up a family,' said Myra, joining the conversation. She paused delicately. 'Are you planning to have children?'

'At least six,' said Pandora, and Ran choked on his scone, spraying crumbs down the front of his shirt. Tutting, she leant across and brushed him down. 'What a mess!' she murmured. Ran's eyes promised vengeance, but, safe in the knowledge that he could hardly say anything with the Americans sitting there, she merely smiled sunnily back at him.

'I guess you have to get used to mess if you're going to have six kids,' said Myra. 'I had four, so I know!'

Pandora was beginning to enjoy herself. She leant forward confidingly. 'I'd like boys, but Ran wants girls just like me. Don't you, darling?'

Ran looked as if he was shuddering at the prospect of six little Pandoras. 'No one could be just like you, Pandora,' he said.

'Is this your wedding photo?' Elaine interrupted, picking the photograph up off the side table next to her. 'I don't remember noticing it before.'

'Really?' said Ran casually. 'I'm surprised you didn't see it. It was one of the first things I unpacked when I got here.'

Pandora eyed him almost admiringly. He was a much better liar than she was. She was sure that neither Elaine nor Myra had the slightest suspicion that he had only taken the picture out of its box that morning.

'It's lovely,' Elaine declared, looking from the laughing faces in the photograph to Ran and Pandora sitting

side by side on the sofa. 'You look so happy together.'
She handed it across to Myra, who nodded.

'Some couples never look as if they really belong
together, but you two do.'

Pandora didn't dare look at Ran, but she could sense
him stiffen at the other end of the sofa, and she
stiffened in turn at his obvious revulsion at the idea.

Myra was still admiring the photograph. 'It looks
quite a recent picture. You haven't been married long,
have you?'

'Sometimes it feels like just a day,' said Pandora,
with a barbed glance at Ran, who bared his teeth back
at her.

'Sometimes it feels like for ever!'

'That's just the way it should be,' said Elaine with a
sentimental sigh. 'Pandora was telling us that you didn't
hit it off at all when you first met.'

'No,' said Ran with something of a snap. 'I thought
she was the most exasperating female I'd ever had the
misfortune to come across!'

'And I've told Myra and Elaine how pompous and
arrogant and insufferable *you* were, *darling*,' said
Pandora, sugar-sweet.

The Americans laughed heartily. 'I guess you've
changed your minds!'

Pandora could see Ran struggling to bite back a
stinging retort. He was obviously longing to tell them
that she had only ever confirmed his opinion of her,
and, prompted by a spirit of pure mischief, she slid
across the sofa and rested her cheek winsomely against
his shoulder. 'Of course he has!' she said, deliberately
excluding herself. She cast a glance up at him from
under her lashes and was delighted to see the muscle
hammering in his clenched jaw. 'Haven't you, darling?'

'Of course I have,' he agreed between his teeth, but

seized the first opportunity to sweep Pandora and the tea-tray out of the room so that they could argue properly.

'What the hell was all that about?' he demanded as soon as the kitchen door had swung to behind them.

'All what?' said Pandora innocently as she tried to calm Homer, who had been shut in the scullery over tea and was now carrying on as if he had been released from a lifetime's incarceration.

'You know perfectly well what!' said Ran, crashing the cups and saucers down beside the sink. 'That simpering little bride act. "Of course he's changed his mind,"' he mimicked her savagely. 'Chance would be a fine thing!'

Pandora gave Homer the last scone and handed the plate to Ran, licking the crumbs off her fingers. 'You said you wanted me to act like a wife,' she pointed out.

'Was calling me "darling" and smirking up at me under your lashes the best you could do?'

'At least I was better than you!' she said crossly. 'You're hardly a great loss to the acting profession, are you? New husbands aren't supposed to look appalled every time their brides come near them. Myra and Elaine must have wondered what was wrong with you; you looked as if you'd found something under a stone.'

'Don't exaggerate!'

'I'm not exaggerating!' Pandora banged the washing-up bowl into the sink and squeezed in three times as much liquid as was necessary. 'I'd have got a warmer response if I'd cuddled up to that bear in the hall!'

'I didn't notice you complaining earlier,' he said nastily, and a tide of colour swept up Pandora's throat to stain her cheeks. It was unfair of him to remind her of that kiss now, just when she was comfortably cross. She didn't want to remember the hot rush of desire, the dark, dangerous excitement of his lips on hers, his hard body pressing her back against the wall.

'I'm not complaining,' she said in a stiff voice. Unable to look at him, she watched the water gushing into the plastic bowl instead. 'You're the one who wants to convince them that we're married, not me. There's no point in me pretending to be an affectionate wife if you're going to look exasperated whenever you see me.'

'It might be easier if you didn't *make* me exasperated!' Ran had been glowering at her averted face, but now he raked his fingers through his hair and turned away with a short sigh. 'All right, we'll both try harder this evening,' he said abruptly. 'They don't seem to be suspicious so far, so if we can just get through to breakfast we should be all right. With any luck, this time tomorrow the whole ghastly farce will be over. No doubt you're as anxious as I am to get on with your own life.'

Was she? Pandora couldn't remember what her own life *was* any more. Time before she had met Ran had taken on a blurry quality. What had she thought about before that vase crashed to the floor and he crashed into her life? Presumably she had been happy with Homer and her pottery, but it all seemed curiously blank now, as if she had been living in a negative which had only been developed into full colour when Ran had appeared. Would life go back to black and white after he left?

Pandora felt chill at the thought. He was scarcely more than a stranger, and already it was impossible to imagine life without him. Who would she argue with? Who would infuriate her and provoke her and make her bones dissolve just by turning his head?

She had her exhibition. Pandora clung to the idea.

Wasn't that what she had worked for and longed for for as long as she could remember? Why should the prospect seem less exciting just because Ran would be going back to Africa and Cindy?

'Yes,' she said, dismayed to hear the doubt in her own voice. Tomorrow, her debt would be paid. Tomorrow, she could concentrate on the exhibition. Tomorrow, she could walk out of here and never see Ran Masterson again. 'Of course I am.'

While Ran gave Myra and Elaine an exhaustive tour of the house and grounds, Pandora tried to organise dinner, but she kept forgetting what she was supposed to be doing as her mind veered between the prospect of life without Ran and the prospect of a night *with* him. If only he weren't so disturbing. If only she didn't keep remembering the feel of his hands and the hardness of his body and the tantalising promise of his mouth.

Pandora caught herself up and added a third spoonful of salt to the potatoes. She must stop this! She must think about how much she still had to do for the exhibition, think of how she was going to stop Homer chewing all her shoes, think about anything except what it would be like to lie near Ran in the dark and listen to him breathing.

The kitchen looked as if the proverbial bomb had hit it when Ran came back later. Pandora had been attempting to thicken the sauce for the chicken with a flour and butter paste and was frantically trying to stir out the resulting lumps, but she looked round when she heard the door open.

Ran was standing there in evening dress, and for once her heart didn't give that sickening lurch. Instead it cartwheeled around her chest like an Olympic gymnast, springing and swinging and pirouetting out of

control. The wooden spoon dropped from her fingers
to slide slowly down into the sauce unnoticed. Ran in
casual shirt and trousers was disturbing enough, but
Ran in a dinner jacket was overwhelming. The severity
of black and white suited his austere features, and he
looked dark and cool and unnervingly attractive.
Pandora gulped.

'What's the matter?' he asked, frowning at her
expression.

'Nothing,' she croaked. Turning back to the cooker,
she bent her head over the boiling sauce and tried to
fish out the spoon, which was almost entirely submerged. 'I. . .er. . .didn't realise we were going to be so
formal this evening, that's all.'

'Myra and Elaine are sounding more and more
enthusiastic,' Ran told her. 'If we pull out all the stops
tonight, I think we'll clinch it. That means you making
an attempt to glam yourself up a bit too.'

'I haven't got time,' said Pandora, whipping out the
spoon at last and dropping it on the side so that she
could suck her scalded fingers. 'There's still too much
to do down here.'

'It doesn't matter if dinner's a bit late. It's more
important that you don't look a mess.' He glanced
around the chaotic kitchen. 'I'll try and clear up here
while Elaine and Myra are changing,' he said. 'If I can.'

Having asked for a bag of clay, Pandora remembered
being disappointed when her mother had insisted on
giving her the grey dress for her last birthday. She
couldn't imagine when she would wear it, but her
mother had pointed out that she never knew when she
would be invited to a formal occasion, and then she
would be glad that she had a dress that didn't date.
And now she was.

It was very simply cut, with a low neckline that left

her shoulders bare and a soft skirt falling from a tailored waist. The beauty lay in the texture of the material, which was a plain, silvery grey, and gave her skin a subtle lustre. Pandora turned in front of the mirror, inspecting herself dubiously. She didn't look right in evening dress, she decided, oblivious to the fact that the design set off the pure lines of her throat and shoulders. The pale grey looked wonderful with her cloud of soft, dark hair and her wide violet eyes, but Pandora saw only that she didn't look capable or efficient or any of the things that Cindy was supposed to be.

In need of extra confidence, she pulled her hair away from her face and piled it on top of her head. No matter how many grips she used, stray wisps kept falling down, and the end result was a little lopsided, but she thought she looked a little more sophisticated. Not much, but a little.

The diamonds on her left hand winked and glimmered distractingly. Pandora looked down at the rings, remembering the brush of Ran's fingers as he'd slid them on, the feel of his hand holding hers still, and something uncoiled itself deep inside her before she managed to jerk her eyes away. Her fingers weren't quite steady as she fixed her grandmother's pearl drop earrings into her ears. It was obviously the night for wearing your grandmother's jewellery.

When she looked at herself in the mirror, her eyes looked huge and vulnerable. She was nervous of going downstairs, she realised. She was nervous of standing near Ran and wondering what it would be like to lean against him and touch her lips to the corner of his mouth and feel him smile.

'Don't even *think* about it,' Pandora told her reflection out loud. She was repaying a debt, that was all.

She would go downstairs, she would be pleasant and charming, she would come up here and sleep on the sofa and then it would all be over. Easy. She smiled at herself in the mirror. It was meant to be confident but succeeded only in looking very, very doubtful.

Well, she couldn't stay up here all night. Pandora went across to the door and took hold of the handle. It would be easy, she told herself again, then, taking a deep breath, she opened the door and walked down the stairs.

CHAPTER SEVEN

PANDORA hesitated by the stuffed python at the foot of the stairs. The door to Ran's study stood ajar and the sound of voices came from inside. She walked over resolutely, only to stop at the last minute on the pretext of adjusting the neckline of her dress, then, when she couldn't put it off any longer, she pushed open the door.

The study was flooded with the evening light that poured golden through the tall French windows. It dazzled her eyes after the gloomy hall and she faltered in the doorway as the others turned. For a moment, nobody spoke. Pandora stood there, blinking in the sunshine, unconscious of the picture she made, enveloped in light, with her dark hair escaping from its pins and the pearls trembling below her ears.

'Is everything all right?' she asked, puzzled by their silence, and Ran cleared his throat.

'We were just wondering where you were,' he said, but his voice sounded strained.

'You look *beautiful*,' said Elaine warmly. 'Doesn't she, Ran?'

Ran looked at Pandora. 'Yes,' he said, handing her a glass of wine. 'Very.'

Her fingers brushed against his as she took the glass from him, but she didn't meet his eyes. It was obvious that he didn't mean it. He was just saying that because they would think it peculiar if he pointed out, as he was no doubt longing to do, that her hair was falling all over her face and that she looked just as messy as usual.

'I love your earrings, too,' Myra said, peering at them.

Pandora touched them so that they swung and shimmered. 'They were my grandmother's.'

'It's so nice to see a grandmother's jewellery being worn instead of put away in a box,' said Myra, and Pandora couldn't help glancing down at the rings on her hand and then up—fleetingly—at Ran.

'Yes, I think so too.'

'They're unusual, aren't they?' Elaine had come over to admire the earrings as well. 'I must say, you've got a style all of your own, Pandora.'

Across the room, Pandora saw Ran splutter into his drink. She didn't blame him. No one had ever called her stylish before. She stared at Elaine. 'I *have*?'

'Oh, yes. We were remarking on it earlier. Take that dress you were wearing when we arrived. It looked soft and comfortable and sort of faded, and yet it was just right for a house like this.'

'Well, I suppose there isn't much point in power dressing when you've got a stuffed bear in the hall,' Pandora murmured, still rather baffled.

'Exactly! But you can obviously look very classy when you need to—like now.'

'Or at your wedding,' Myra put in. 'That hat! What style!'

'Hat?' said Pandora cautiously. How on earth did they know about the hat? She wasn't wearing it in the photograph Ran had had developed for the drawing room.

'This one.' Myra picked up a framed photograph from the mantelpiece and flourished it at Pandora.

There she was, chin tilted, face half-hidden by the enormous rim, managing to look both sparkling and defiant. Pandora stared at herself. Why did Ran have a picture of her in here? Of course, it was just the kind of detail that he would think of, but even so. . .

Almost reluctantly, her eyes met Ran's. They were as inscrutable as ever. 'That's funny,' she said slowly to Myra, although she was still looking directly at him. 'I always used to think Ran loathed that hat.'

'I did,' he said, answering the question she hadn't asked. 'But when you weren't here, and I used to think about you, it was always as you looked when you were wearing that hat.'

Pandora could feel a blush start deep inside her, spreading out until it tingled over her bare shoulders and burned in her cheeks. 'Isn't it hot in here?' she said hurriedly. 'Why don't we take our drinks outside?'

Ran pushed open the French windows and they spilled out onto the terrace. Of course, it *would* have to be the very place where he had kissed her! Elaine and Myra made a beeline for the stone lions at the top of the steps. 'Oh, I just *love* these lions!' Myra cried, patting the head of the very one. 'Just think of how long they've been sitting here, and what they've seen and heard!'

Out of the corner of her eye, Pandora saw Ran's mouth twitch and knew that he was thinking of exactly what the lions had seen only yesterday afternoon. Her chin went up fractionally. 'Do you think so?' she said. 'I've always thought them rather overrated myself.'

'Oh?' said Ran, taking up the challenge. 'I thought you loved them.' His eyes rested significantly on the lion's back where a patch of moss was crushed and crumbling. 'Especially this one.'

'Well, I didn't!' she was provoked into retorting. 'I mean, I don't.'

'I suppose after living in Africa you're used to seeing real lions,' Elaine commented.

'Oh, all the time,' Pandora invented breezily and Ran looked annoyed.

'No, *not* all the time. As you've probably gathered, Pandora's given to exaggeration at times,' he added in an audible aside to the Americans. 'In fact we live— *lived*—in the capital, and there aren't many lions roaming around the street there.'

'But we saw hundreds when you took me out on safari to propose, didn't we?' Pandora put in naughtily.

'Some,' he amended with a quelling look.

Thrilled, Myra clasped her hands together. 'Weren't you frightened being out in the bush with all those wild animals, Pandora?'

'I'm never frightened when Ran's with me,' said Pandora, the picture of innocence.

'It must have been wonderful!'

'Oh, it was,' she said. 'In fact, now that I'm here, it all seems like a dream. Sometimes it's as if I've never really been there at all.'

She smiled at Elaine and Myra who nodded understandingly. Catching Ran's eye, she saw that he was torn between exasperation and amusement, and although he shook his head at her in reproof he gave in and grinned reluctantly in the end. Pandora, feeling that she had won that round, grinned back, and although they weren't even standing near each other for a few seconds they were alone together, bound by a moment of shared complicity and humour.

The Americans were admiring the view out across the sweep of lawn to the great beeches and chestnut trees, and Elaine had her camera out. 'The light's perfect,' she enthused. 'Everything's so peaceful.'

Pandora felt anything but peaceful when Myra suggested that her partner take a picture of her and Ran together. 'It would make such a nice shot with the two of you together by the lion.'

'Well, I really need to see about the dinner...' she said, putting her wineglass down on the balustrade and edging back towards the study.

'It won't take a second,' Elaine promised gaily.

'Come here and be nice, Pandora,' said Ran, with more than a hint of steel behind his polite smile. He moved over to the lion and held out his hand.

Pandora had little choice but to pin a smile to her face and stand stiffly next to him.

'A little closer!' called Elaine from behind the camera.

Without fuss, Ran put his arm around Pandora's waist and pulled her against him. 'Like this?'

'That looks nice and relaxed... Smile!'

It didn't feel relaxed. It felt alarming, unnerving, heart-shaking—anything *but* relaxed. Ran stood easily smiling, but his arm was like a bar of steel holding her into his side. His body was a tempting rock, spare and solid and utterly controlled. Pandora's eyes were on a level with his throat. She could see the pulse beating slow and steady below his ear and was shaken by a sudden, terrible desire to relax into him, to press her face into his throat and breathe in his cool, reassuring strength.

Terrified that she would give in to the temptation, Pandora turned and smiled resolutely at the camera.

At last it was over, and Ran released her, letting his hand slide leisurely down her back. Immediately, she felt lopsided without him to lean against. 'I'd better go and see what's happening in the kitchen,' she muttered, and fled.

*   *   *

In the end, the dinner wasn't as bad as Pandora had feared. The fish mousse hadn't quite set, but her artist's eye stood her in good stead, and she was able to disguise most of its shortcomings with clever decoration. As for the chicken, it looked absolutely nothing like the recipe, but once she had sieved the lumps out of the sauce it was really quite tasty. The lemon tart, it had to be admitted, was such a disaster that Pandora threw it into the bin and arranged a display of fresh fruit on each plate instead.

Sitting at the end of the table, Pandora felt by the end of the meal that she had brushed through the cooking pretty well. Myra and Elaine had seemed to enjoy the food, although that might have had more to do with the wonderful wine that Ran had discovered down in the cellar, and even he had looked approving.

At the other end of the table, he was looking urbane, even distinguished, in the dark jacket, and the white shirt was positively dazzling against his bronzed skin. Pandora had always thought of him as a man that belonged in a wide, empty space, where the horizon shimmered through the heat and the dust, but suddenly she saw him for what he was: a man equally at home sitting around government tables, cutting through bureaucracy, making sure things got done, not next year, not next week, but now, when they were needed.

A man who worked best on his own, uncluttered by the commitments of a wife and family. A man who had made no secret of the fact that he would walk away from here as soon as he could and not look back.

Why couldn't she remember *that* instead of how warm and enticing his touch had been this afternoon? She should be thinking about leaving tomorrow confident in the knowledge that her debt had been paid in full, not about the spinning excitement of his kiss or the hard strength of his body or the way her bones seemed to melt whenever he smiled.

But then, perhaps it was better than thinking about sharing a room with him tonight. Every time Pandora thought about the night to come, her nerves jarred. She was vexed with herself for getting in such a state about it. Ran had assured her that he wouldn't lay a finger on her; why couldn't she accept that and relax?

Because he had kissed her.

Because he had smiled at her across the hall.

Because she could remember every time he had touched her.

Myra was enthusing about the local countryside. 'This is such a beautiful area! We had no idea. Neither of us has ever been to Northumberland before, so we're real keen to explore.'

'We drove through Wickworth today,' Elaine chipped in. 'It looked like just the kind of place our clients like to discover for themselves. We provide a sort of guide to the local area for them when they book,' she explained to them. 'We were thinking we might stay around here for a while and see what else we could find to recommend.'

'We do so much travelling that we hardly ever get to see anywhere properly. It would be such a treat to stay in one place for a change.' Myra was a study in artlessness as she looked from Ran to Pandora. 'I wonder, could you recommend anywhere nice for us to stay?'

There was an awkward pause. Ran looked at Pandora and Pandora looked at Ran, but both knew that there was only one answer.

'You must stay here, of course,' he said pleasantly, only a slight rigidity of the jaw betraying his consternation.

'Oh, we couldn't impose. . .'

'Nonsense. We'd be delighted to have you, wouldn't we, darling?'

Pandora made a heroic effort to conceal her dismay. 'Of course we would.'

'There is only one problem,' he went on, and she crossed her fingers under the table, hoping that this was his way of dissuading the Americans. 'Pandora's got an important exhibition coming up soon, so she's going to be very busy over the next week or so.'

Then, of course, she had to explain all about her pottery and the exhibition, and just hope that it wouldn't occur to them to wonder how she had managed to arrange and produce enough for an exhibition in the short time she was supposed to have been here. Fortunately neither of them knew anything about pottery, but they were alarmingly interested—so much so that they bombarded her with questions for a good half an hour, until Ran tactfully suggested that they retire for the night. The clearing-up, he said, could wait until the morning.

'It's only a small local exhibition,' said Pandora desperately as they made their way upstairs and the women began to talk about staying to support her.

'Still, we'd love to see it—if you don't mind, of course. It would be so lovely to stay here for a while. We won't be any trouble. We'll be out all day looking around, and we can easily eat out if that makes things any easier, so you won't have to do anything for us.'

'Only stay married,' muttered Ran as they finally managed to say goodnight to the exhaustingly grateful Americans on the landing and shut the bedroom door.

'It's your fault,' said Pandora accusingly, so edgy at the prospect of continuing this farce for another ten days that she had quite forgotten the awkwardness of disappearing into a bedroom with him 'You invited them!'

'I didn't have much choice,' he pointed out, pulling off his tie. 'They were dropping such heavy hints that I could hardly ignore them.'

'You could have thought of something!'

'Like what?'

'I don't know,' she admitted sulkily. 'It didn't take you long to think up a wife when you needed one. I'd have thought some excuse about why they couldn't stay would have been a doddle after that!'

'In that case, why didn't you say anything?' he retorted irritably. 'I'm not exactly over the moon at the idea either, but it's too late to do anything about it now.' He took off his jacket and sat down on the edge of the bed to untie his shoe laces. 'We'll just have to put up with it. It'll only be for a few days, after all.'

'Ten!' Too restless to sit down, Pandora paced around the room. 'And what if they want to stay longer? They might be here for weeks. At this rate, we'll have to stay married for ever!'

'Don't you think you're overreacting?' said Ran, watching her as he unfastened his cuffs. 'We'll certainly have to stay married for as long as they're here, but if they look like staying too long your mother can have a relapse and you can rush down to her side.'

'I can't just disappear! I've got an exhibition in ten days' time and I've got far too much to do as it is.'

'You'll still be able to work during the day,' he pointed out, infuriatingly reasonable. 'They'll take themselves off after breakfast every day, so you'll have plenty of time while they're out. Stop making such a fuss! All it means is that you'll have to sleep here instead of at the stables.'

Pandora sank down abruptly at the dressing table

and began pulling the grips from her hair with agitated fingers. 'All?' she echoed. '*All*? I've got to carry on pretending to be in love with you, carry on sharing a room with a virtual stranger, and you tell me I'm making a fuss!'

'I won't be a stranger after you've been sleeping with me for a while,' said Ran with one of his disquieting gleams of humour. He swung his legs up on the bed and settled back against the pillows with his hands behind his head.

'I've no intention of sleeping with you!' snapped Pandora, yanking out the last grip and slamming it down onto the dressing table. The whole absurd situation had completely unnerved her. Contemplating one night with Ran had been bad enough, but now it looked as if she was going to have to get through another week!

Ran sighed. 'I don't know what you're so worried about, Pandora. I'm quite capable of keeping my hands off you.'

'That wasn't the impression I got this afternoon.'

'It won't happen again,' he said, holding up crossed fingers in mock apology. 'Scout's honour!' His cool gaze rested on Pandora, who was edgily taking out her earrings. 'Unless you ask, of course,' he added as an afterthought.

Pandora's fingers froze at her ear as her eyes met Ran's in the mirror. She could see him lying back on the bed, looking dark and amused and annoyingly relaxed, his shirt unfastened to reveal the strong column of his neck and the first dark hairs on his chest, and she had a sudden, horrifyingly clear picture of turning on the stool and smiling, of crossing the room to let him pull her down onto the bed, of unbuttoning the rest of his shirt and sliding her hands around him and asking—begging—him to kiss her again.

Appalled at the vividness of the scene, Pandora stood up jerkily. 'Don't hold your breath,' she said, but her mouth was dry and her voice wasn't nearly as steady as she would have liked. Gathering up her things, she marched out and along to the bathroom before her imagination went any further.

When she came back, she was wearing one of Celia's old-fashioned nightdresses which she had borrowed for the night. It was far too hot, but it had the advantage of a high neck and long sleeves, and Pandora felt safe inside its voluminous folds.

'Very modest,' Ran commented drily, amused by her attempt to ignore him as she hung up her dress, the soft hair tumbling to her shoulders and the beautiful eyes defiant and more than a little wary. 'But make sure you don't stand with the light behind you, or I'll be able to see right through it!'

Blushing furiously, Pandora whisked herself out of the light and marched round to the other side of the bed.

He didn't move. 'Don't tell me that you've changed your mind about sharing?'

'No, I haven't!' she said, seizing a pillow and attempting to tug the eiderdown from beneath him. 'If you were a gentleman, you wouldn't even suggest such a thing!'

'Stop talking like something out of a bad novel, Pandora!' said Ran dampeningly. 'This is the twentieth century, the bed is more than big enough for two of us and I don't see why I should spend an uncomfortable night on the sofa just because you won't believe I'm not panting after your body.'

'Fine!' said Pandora with freezing dignity. 'If that's the way you feel, I shall sleep on the sofa, that's all.'

Rolling his eyes, Ran raised himself slightly so that she could snatch the eiderdown away at last. 'You'll be extremely uncomfortable,' he warned.

'Not as uncomfortable as I'd be sharing a bed with you!' she retorted, stalking over to the sofa and throwing her pillow down on it.

It wasn't long, though, before she began to regret the stand she had taken. The leather sofa was even more uncomfortable than Ran had warned. It was hard and lumpy and rose up in a sort of hillock in the middle so that Pandora kept falling down the slope towards the floor. She couldn't stretch out properly either, and had to try and arrange herself around the bumps, but it was impossible to get comfortable. The window was open to the warm June night, but she was still far too hot, even when she had discarded the eiderdown. To make matters worse, she kept getting tangled up in the long nightgown, and every time she moved to free her legs the leather shrieked in protest.

'For God's sake!' Ran's irritable sigh came out of the darkness when this had been going on for half an hour. 'Can't you lie still?'

'I can't get comfortable,' she said sullenly, banging her pillow into a new shape.

'If you stopped playing the martyr and got into bed, you'd soon get comfortable.'

'No, thank you,' she said in frosty accents.

'Well, in that case, would you please lie still and then at least one of us can get some sleep?'

Pandora willed herself not to move. She lay on her back, staring up at the ceiling and trying to ignore the lump that was digging into her shoulder, but it was no good. When she could bear it no longer, she shifted very cautiously, and the sofa immediately creaked as if she had jumped up and down on it. She held her breath, but there was no sound from the bed.

Surely Ran hadn't fallen asleep? She threw herself onto her side but there was still no response. He *had* fallen asleep! Simmering with fury at the idea of him sleeping soundly while she was so uncomfortable, Pandora lay awake, tossing restlessly, hot and aching and tormented by thoughts of being able to stretch out on a firm mattress only feet away. She was so tired that she dozed off every now and then, only to jerk awake as she found herself sliding off the sofa. The fourth time it happened, she didn't have time to disentangle herself from the nightgown and ended up on the floor with a loud thump.

A light clicked on by Ran's bedside. Without saying a word, he threw back the sheet, walked over to where Pandora lay still sprawled in an undignified heap on the carpet, picked her up bodily and carried her over to the bed where he dumped her without ceremony.

'What are you doing?' she protested, as breathless from the contact with his bare chest as from her fall.

'I am *trying* to get some sleep,' said Ran, collecting her pillow and shoving it into her hands. 'And as neither of us is going to get any with you crashing around on that sofa I suggest you swallow your pride and accept your share of the bed. I don't care whether you lie on top of the sheet or put pillows down the middle, but whatever you do do it quietly and for God's sake stop wriggling!'

Then he walked back round to his side of the bed, switched off the light and calmly got in beside her. Pandora lay rigid and tried to get her breath back. For a while she contemplated marching back to the sofa in high dudgeon, but there was no doubt that the bed was

a lot more comfortable, and when Ran turned his back
to her and fell asleep with obnoxious ease she allowed
her stiff body to relax slightly.

He had been right. There was plenty of room for
them both. She wasn't touching him at all, but she was
still very conscious of his warm, lean body only inches
from hers. Moonlight striped the bed through the open
window. Ran lay in its shadows, but where it glanced
off his shoulder Pandora could see the sheen of his skin
and flexing of his powerful muscles when he stirred in
his sleep. She had clutched at him instinctively when
he'd swooped her up from the floor and she could still
feel the sleek strength of his shoulders beneath her
hands.

She wished she could discard her nightdress and lie
like Ran, letting the night air whisper cool over her
skin. It would be lovely to lie in this wide bed and not
feel the tension twisting inside her, to be able to roll
over and lay her hand against his back and feel him
breathing.

Pandora's fingers prickled, and she rolled over to
face firmly away from temptation, but it didn't make
much difference. She still vibrated with his nearness,
with the knowledge of how easy it would be to turn
and touch him. Images chased themselves across her
mind—of Ran shaking his head at her in exasperation,
Ran pressing her against the kitchen wall, Ran holding
her against his side and letting his hand drift slowly
down her back.

She would have been better off staying on the sofa,
Pandora decided despairingly. She'd *known* it would
be like this. At this rate she wouldn't get any sleep
until Myra and Elaine left.

Gradually, though, the sound of Ran's slow, steady
breathing began to soothe her frazzled nerves and her

mind drifted as the reassurance of his sleeping presence seeped through her. There was something hypnotic about his even breaths, and she fell asleep at last, still listening to them.

The dawn light through the open curtains woke her briefly, and she lay for a while, blinking at the light and filled with a sense of well-being. It was only slowly that she became conscious of an unaccustomed weight on her, and she looked sleepily down to see Ran's arm thrown across her body. He was lying on his front, his face turned towards her on the pillow and the watchful expression relaxed in sleep.

It was very early. Outside, only the birds were awake and busy, shouting and twittering at each other in the trees. She let her hand slide almost absently down the arm that lay across her, savouring the coiled, compact strength of the muscles, rubbing her thumb over the dark hairs on his forearm, circling her fingers over his skin.

To Pandora, adrift between sleep and the dawn, it seemed perfectly natural to be lying there close to him, feeling him breathe against her. Somewhere, a voice was urging her to move away, but she was too sleepy and too comfortable to listen, and she closed her eyes instead, turning instinctively into the security of his body.

When she woke again, Ran was gone. Pandora stretched and then jerked upright as her mind cleared and she realised where she was. She remembered falling off the lumpy sofa, and Ran's exasperation as he had picked her up. She remembered the feel of his bare chest and shoulders, and the way he had dumped her on the bed...but surely it had been on the other side? What was she doing on Ran's side of the bed?

Pandora sat up and pushed the tousled hair out of

her eyes, spreading her hands over the sheet as if there
were some way of telling if she had spent the whole
night there, or if she had only rolled over unconsciously
once Ran had left. She hoped it was the latter. She had
a vague, disquieting memory of lying against him that
was instantly suppressed. That must have been a
dream. If she *had* woken to find his arm across her, she
would have moved away, not turned towards him.

Wouldn't she?

She found Ran making fresh coffee in the kitchen
and grumbling at Homer who kept getting under his
feet. Pandora felt ridiculously awkward about facing
him, but he gave absolutely no sign that they had even
spent the night together, and if she had snuggled into
his arms in her sleep the experience had obviously left
him completely unmoved.

'At last!' he said, looking up as she came into the
kitchen. 'I thought you were going to sleep all
morning.'

'It's only half past seven!' Homer had bounded over
to greet her enthusiastically and Pandora bent to rub
his shaggy head. It was certainly too early to start
arguing. 'What time did you get up?'

'Six,' said Ran. He was wearing grey trousers and a
short-sleeved white shirt, and looked cool and crisp
and—yes—as if he had been awake for hours. 'You
were dead to the world, so you obviously got over the
trauma of sharing a bed.' The grey eyes were unnervingly light as he glanced across at her. 'When I woke
up you looked quite at home!'

Pandora wanted to ask him if she had been tangled
against him, but didn't have the nerve. Perhaps it would
be better not to know. 'I can't say I felt at home when
I woke up,' she said.

'You will do by the time Myra and Elaine leave,'

said Ran unsympathetically. 'In the meantime, perhaps we could get to sleep with a little less fuss every night?'

Over breakfast, the Americans announced that they were going off to Bamburgh and wouldn't be back until evening. 'We'll have lunch out, so please don't feel you have to go to any trouble about dinner.'

'They'll still want something,' said Pandora worriedly as they waved Myra and Elaine off. 'We'd better go shopping again.'

'You go back to your pottery,' said Ran. 'I'll sort something out.'

She looked at him in surprise. 'Don't you want me to cook something again tonight?'

'I thought you were desperate to get on with your exhibition?'

'Well, yes, I am, but. . .' Pandora was frankly puzzled by his consideration. 'Aren't you going to remind me how much that vase was worth and how I've got off so lightly so far?'

'That wasn't what you said last night,' said Ran drily, and she flushed, remembering the scene she had made about sleeping on the sofa.

'I was just expecting you to claim the next ten days as part of my debt, that's all.'

'We agreed that you would help me convince Myra and Elaine that you were my wife, and I expect you to see that through. Given that you've got an exhibition to prepare, I don't think it's fair to expect you to carry on with the cooking as well.'

'Oh. . .well. . .thank you,' she said awkwardly. Turning, they walked back up the steps to the front door. 'Does that mean you're going to have a go at cooking after all?'

'No, Pandora, it does not,' said Ran firmly. 'A nice

woman from the village has been coming in three days
a week to help me out, so I'll ask her to come every
day to keep things tidy and prepare the meals. I didn't
really want her around when Myra and Elaine were
here, but since we've already told them about your
exhibitions they'll probably understand.'

Pandora thought. 'What will you tell her about us?'

'I'll tell her the truth. She's very discreet, and Myra
and Elaine are likely to be out when she's around
anyway.'

'It sounds perfect,' said Pandora, then hesitated.
'Won't you mind paying her when you'd probably be
justified in asking me to do the work for free?'

Ran looked amused. 'Anyone would think you
wanted to carry on as housekeeper!'

'I don't,' she said. 'I just. . .well, I suppose I still feel
a bit guilty.'

'Don't,' he said briskly. 'Nancy is an excellent cook
and needs the work. You've kept your part of the
agreement as far as the cooking goes, and I don't want
to be held responsible for jeopardising a promising
artistic reputation if you don't get everything ready in
time for your exhibition! Besides,' he went on with an
ironic look, 'you're going to have enough to do pretending to be a sweet, loving wife, so if you must feel
guilty concentrate on that!'

CHAPTER EIGHT

THE studio was very quiet. Pandora sat on the stool and ran her finger around the edge of the wheel. She felt as if she had been away for years and was both surprised and reassured on coming home to find that everything was exactly the same as she remembered.

Unable to settle, she prowled around the room, picking up the pieces she had completed, able for the first time to study them with an impersonal eye. They were good, she decided in a detached way—the best that she had ever done. Why couldn't she feel more excited about them?

Ran had taken Homer down to the village with him to see Nancy about the cooking. 'It's high time this dog had some discipline,' he had said. 'He can come with me and learn some obedience.' Perhaps that was why the studio felt so empty? Pandora caught herself up as she sighed. A peaceful studio, no distractions, no wondering where Homer was or what he was doing. . . what more did she want? She should be making the most of this time, not mooning around thinking about a man and a dog.

The pots in the trays were leather-hard and right for turning. One by one, Pandora turned them upside down on the wheel and carved off the excess clay with a turning tool. Once she had got into the rhythm, it was easy, and she got through the tray in record time, relieved to find that she could concentrate after all.

Occasionally her mind would drift off to picture the narrow country lane that led the two miles to the

village. Ran would be striding purposefully along,
Homer bounding beside him in the sunshine, the man
contained and controlled, the dog unruly and uncoor-
dinated. Pandora smiled to think of them together, but
when she found that she had been sitting and smiling
down at the same pot for quarter of an hour she hastily
called her thoughts to order.

She worked so well that she lost all track of time,
and when Homer bustled excitably into the studio she
was astonished to see that it was half past one. 'Hello,
boy,' she said, bending down to pat him and smiling at
his wrigglingly enthusiastic welcome. 'What have you
done with Ran?'

'He's driven me to distraction, that's what he's done,'
said Ran, appearing in the doorway.

Pandora was still smiling as she glanced up. As
always when she saw him, her heart seemed to turn
over, and her smile faltered slightly but she managed
to keep her voice steady. 'Oh, dear, has he been
naughty?'

'Naughty? Possessed by devils would be closer to the
mark,' he said astringently. 'I've been trying to teach
him some basic obedience.' He whistled to demon-
strate, and Homer rushed back over to him, wagging
his tail. 'Sit!'

Homer promptly dropped to the floor and rolled
sycophantically over onto his back. Pandora laughed.
'Well, it's better than nothing,' she said, and although
Ran tried to look severe he shook his head and
crouched down to pat the dog's tummy.

'Hopeless!' he grinned.

Pandora watched his hand reducing the dog to
squirming ecstasy. Lucky Homer, she found herself
thinking, and looked quickly away.

'I hope he hasn't been too much of a nuisance. Do you want to leave him with me now?'

'Not unless you particularly want him, and I find that hard to believe. He's nearly as distracting as you are.' Ran straightened, and turned to pick up the plate he had put down as he'd come in. 'We just came to bring you some lunch,' he explained. 'I thought if you were working you might appreciate a sandwich.'

'Oh. . .' Ridiculously, Pandora couldn't think of anything to say. She took the plate as if it held the crown jewels, absurdly touched that he had taken the time and trouble to think of her lunch. 'You shouldn't have,' she said inadequately.

'Perhaps it's my way of saying that I'm sorry you've got to carry on pretending to be my wife,' he said gruffly. 'I know you don't like the situation.'

Pandora looked down at the floor. 'It's not that bad,' she muttered.

'Let's just make the best of it, shall we?' said Ran, and at last she raised her eyes to his.

'Yes,' she said.

There was a silence. A strange, quivery feeling began in Pandora's stomach and fluttered outwards. She wanted to look away, but couldn't, and in the end it was Ran who turned away. 'We'd better let you get on. Come on, Homer.' Homer, who had been lying waiting hopefully to have his stomach patted some more, scrambled to his feet and followed Ran to the door.

Pandora watched them go. 'Ran,' she called as he disappeared, and he put his head back round the door. 'Yes?'

'I. . .' How could she tell him how she felt? She didn't know herself any more. 'Thank you for the sandwich,' was all she said in the end, and Ran gave one of his heart-shaking smiles.

'See you later,' he said, and then he was gone.

Pandora washed her hands and sat down at the table, curling up the edge of the sandwich to see the filling. Ham and chutney—her favourite. How had he guessed? Now that she saw it, she was hungry. Perhaps that was what that odd feeling in the pit of her stomach had been. Ran's parting smile burned behind her eyes as she picked up one half of the sandwich in both hands and she thought of him as he had looked crouched beside Homer, amusement tugging at his mouth in spite of his attempt at severity.

'I know you don't like the situation,' he had apologised.

Didn't she? The answer dried the breath in Pandora's throat and she put the sandwich uncertainly back down on the plate. She had been fooling herself all along. She didn't dislike being with Ran at all. She loved being with him. She loved *him*.

'Oh, dear,' she said out loud. Her appetite had abruptly deserted her and she stared miserably down at the sandwich. How could she have allowed herself to fall in love with Ran? They had absolutely nothing in common. He had Cindy. He was leaving as soon as he could. Three very good reasons for not doing anything silly like falling in love with him.

But it was too late. It had been too late the very first time he had touched her.

Now what was she going to do? There was no point in thinking that he had changed just because he had brought her a sandwich and smiled at her. Ran had never made any secret of what his priorities were. The best she could hope for was to get through the next ten days without embarrassing him or herself by letting him guess how she felt. It wouldn't be easy, but she would try.

Reluctant to face Ran again until she was confident that he wouldn't be able to read the truth in her eyes, Pandora lingered in the studio all day. She tried to convince herself that what she felt for him was no more than a passing infatuation and that she would forget him as soon as he went back to Africa, but she knew in her heart that it wasn't true. This was it; this was love at last. It was just her bad luck that she had to go and fall in love with a man who could never, ever love her back.

Pandora's heart contracted, and she dashed her arm across her eyes to stop the prickling tears. Crying would just make things worse. She wouldn't cry. She *wouldn't*!

She was hunched over a teapot, scratching the detail through the slip with ferocious concentration, when Myra and Elaine found her. 'Still working?' they cried. 'You must be exhausted! Ran says you've been in here all day.'

Pandora put down the teapot and forced a smile. If ever she'd needed any acting skills, it was now! 'I've managed to get a lot done.'

'May we see?' They exclaimed with pleasure at the pieces she showed them. 'This is marvellous!' said Elaine, admiring a plate. 'How wonderful to be able to live in a place like this and have such a talent! You are lucky!'

She would still have the place and her talent when Ran had gone, but how much would they mean then? Pandora reminded herself that she would still have more than most people and that would have to be enough. She put away her tools. 'Yes,' she said bleakly. 'I am.'

She was determinedly cheerful all evening. Once or twice she caught Ran looking at her curiously, but he didn't say anything, and fortunately Myra and Elaine were full of their experiences and did most of the talking. The worst part was going to bed. It was virtually the first time that she and Ran had been alone together that evening, and Pandora knew that if he touched her all her carefully built defences would crumble like so much dust.

He didn't. He was brisk and businesslike and turned his back to her as soon as he got into bed. Pandora climbed in beside him and knew that she ought to have been grateful, but his evident lack of interest scraped at her raw heart. Dry-eyed, she lay and watched his back through the darkness and wondered how she could have come to love him so much in such a short time. She ached to be able to slide over and kiss his shoulder, to feel him stir and smile and roll over to take her in his arms, but instead she turned away to her own side of the bed so that he wouldn't see her if she cried in her sleep.

As soon as Myra and Elaine left the next morning, Pandora fled back to the safety of her studio, muttering about loading the kiln for a firing. Homer seemed to be happy with Ran and now that she didn't have to worry about meals either she had much more time to work than she usually did. At this rate she would have everything ready well in advance.

She was standing back surveying her completed pieces and reassessing how much she still had to do when the sound of a car door banging and footsteps in the courtyard made her look round, her heart leaping in spite of all her stern warnings not to at the thought that Ran was here with her lunch again.

Only it wasn't Ran. It was Quentin. Pandora had to fight down a black, bitter wave of disappointment as she greeted him.

'I thought I'd just drop in and see how you were getting on,' said Quentin, kissing her a little too warmly on the cheeks. 'How are you?'

'I'm fine.' Remembering how she had deliberately encouraged him the other day just to provoke Ran, Pandora felt ashamed. She was back to jeans, a sleeveless T-shirt and her worn old cardigan, but Quentin was looking at her as if she was still wearing the yellow dress.

For a while, he enthused over the work she had done. 'You clever girl! This all looks fantastic! Why don't I take the finished pieces back to the gallery with me now, and you can bring the last bits in when they're ready?'

Together they loaded several trays into the back of his car, but Quentin brushed aside her attempts to thank him. 'Anything I can do for you is a pleasure, Pandora,' he said, moving closer. 'You know that, don't you?'

Pandora's heart sank. 'It's very kind of you,' she said weakly.

'I don't want your gratitude,' said Quentin, taking her hands and looking deep into her eyes. 'It was wonderful to have lunch with you the other day,' he said. 'When are we going to do it again?'

This was all her fault for flirting with him in front of Ran! Somehow, she was going to have to tell him it was all a terrible mistake. 'Quentin, I—'

'Am I interrupting something?' The voice behind them was like a steel trap snapping shut and Pandora snatched her hands away from Quentin, her cheeks aflame. Ran was standing at the courtyard entrance looking murderous. He held a plate of sandwiches in his hand but plainly wished that it were a sword he could use to run through Quentin on the spot.

Quentin's expression was peeved. 'Actually, we were having a private conversation.'

'It looked a damned sight too private to me,' snapped Ran.

'I fail to see that it's any of your business,' said Quentin, then took a step back when he read the menace in Ran's eyes.

'It is when you're having that private a conversation with my wife,' he said dangerously.

'Your *wife*?' Shocked, Quentin turned to stare at Pandora. 'I thought you were here on your own?'

'I was—' Pandora began before Ran interrupted her.

'Pandora and I have had a few problems,' he said in a cold voice. 'She came up here for a trial separation, but we've decided to work things out together. Haven't we?' he added meaningfully to Pandora, who was beginning to look hunted.

'Sort of,' she said.

'I see,' said Quentin stiffly. 'In that case, I'm sorry if I misread the situation.'

'It was my fault,' she said miserably, and Ran glowered. 'Will. . .will this affect the exhibition?'

'Of course not. It's going to be brilliant.' Quentin glanced at Ran with dislike, then turned ostentatiously back to Pandora. He had evidently decided that all hope was not lost. With a husband as unpleasant as Ran, she might well change her mind. 'If there's ever anything I can do for you—anything at all—you know where I am.'

'Thank you.' Pandora felt terrible, but she was anxious for Quentin to leave before Ran turned really nasty. 'I'll bring in the rest of the pieces as soon as I can.'

'I'll look forward to it,' said Quentin provocatively,

and got into his car. 'You're a lucky man,' he said to Ran through the open window.

'I know,' said Ran coldly, and put a deliberate arm around Pandora as they watched Quentin reverse out of the courtyard.

As soon as he had gone, Pandora wrenched herself away. 'You had no business to tell Quentin we were married!'

'He had to know some time,' said Ran indifferently. 'Myra and Elaine are going to the exhibition and who knows who they'll talk to there? I'm not going to ruin everything at the last minute just because of your relationship with Quentin.' He managed to make the name sound like a sneer. 'What did he want anyway? Or can I guess?'

'He came to talk about the exhibition,' said Pandora, tight-lipped.

'Oh, yes? And did he need to hold your hands while he talked about it?' he demanded savagely. 'I'm so sorry to have broken up your little tête-à-tête, but you can hold this instead,' he went on, thrusting the plate of sandwiches into her hand before turning on his heel and striding off.

He never brought her another sandwich after that. The next four days were tense and miserable. Ran and Pandora communicated in monosyllables when they were alone, but put on identically brittle smiles for the Americans, and at night they lay rigid and silent in the big bed.

Pandora spent as much time as she could in the studio, and wondered how it was possible to love someone so much and hate them at the same time. She was furious with Ran for embarrassing her in front of Quentin, and furious with herself for loving him anyway. Ran was just being a dog in the manger. He didn't want her himself, but she wasn't allowed to try and build a life for herself after he had left either. She wouldn't have blamed Quentin if he had told her what she could do with her exhibition after she had apparently lied to him like that, and then where would she have been? No Ran, no exhibition, no nothing.

Pottery was all she was going to have left, and Pandora threw herself into her work, determined to make a success of the exhibition and hoping against hope that if she did Ran would somehow seem less important, his absence less raw.

She wasn't hungry, but every day she went back to the kitchen at Kendrick Hall and made herself a sandwich, just to show Ran that she hadn't lost her appetite and that she didn't care in the least if he never thought about her at lunch time any more. She was crossing the hall on her way back to the studio on the fifth day, when the phone rang in the study. Ran had gone out earlier, Nancy had told her in the kitchen, so Pandora picked up the receiver, knowing even before she heard the voice that it would be Cindy.

It was. Pandora's fingers clenched around the receiver until her knuckles showed white. 'He's out, I'm afraid,' she said tightly when Cindy asked to speak to Ran. 'Can I take a message?'

'No, it's all right.' Cindy's voice was intimidatingly warm and friendly. 'Could you just tell him I rang, and ask him to call me back when he's got a minute? He knows the number.'

Of course he did. He probably knew it off by heart. Pandora put the receiver down slowly. What was the point of wishing and hoping that things would be different? There was obviously nothing wrong between Ran and Cindy, and it was time that she accepted that his future was with the American girl and not with her. She drew the message pad towards her. 'Cindy rang 1:15,' she wrote. 'Please ring her back. I'm taking the rest of my pieces in to Quentin, so will be away all afternoon.' There, that would show him how little she cared!

Quentin was delighted with the final pieces she had brought for the exhibition and tactfully made no reference to the scene with Ran. Pandora spent the afternoon with him, labelling and pricing and trying not to think about Ran on the phone to Cindy. It took longer than she thought and it was nearly seven o'clock before she got back to Kendrick Hall. Everything was very quiet. Myra and Elaine usually came back from their expeditions at about five o'clock, but there was no sign of their car and when Pandora went inside the house was empty and echoing. Ran and Homer must be out too.

Puzzled, she went upstairs to wash and change into a floaty Indian skirt and a worn white top. The last few days had been overcast, in sympathy with her mood, but today the sun had come out again and the air was hot and still, and the soft cottons felt cool and comfortable against her skin. She found herself listening for Ran, but he hadn't reappeared by the time she made her way downstairs, and, feeling rather lost, she wandered into the drawing room.

The room was filled with sunlight just as it had been on the day Myra and Elaine had arrived. Pandora pushed open the windows and as she turned her eye fell on the photograph that Ran had stood on the side table where the Americans would be sure to see it. Picking it up with unsteady hands, she looked down into Ran's smiling face and her heart twisted. They looked so happy, but it had all been an illusion, a trick for the camera.

'So you're back.' Ran's voice startled her so much that she dropped the picture onto the table with a crack, and she flushed as she set it back on its stand. 'What have you been doing with Quentin all this time?'

'Labelling and pricing for the exhibition,' she said, hoping he hadn't seen her gazing down at the photograph.

'Is that all?' he asked as if the words were forced out of him.

'Yes.' Pandora moved away from the table. The air was jangling with tension and her hands felt empty and awkward. She folded them into her arms. 'Where is everybody?' she asked stiltedly.

'Elaine rang up about an hour ago. Apparently they've found some restaurant they want to try and won't be back until late.' Ran prowled over to the fireplace. 'They also think they're being tactful in giving us some time alone together.'

'Oh.' Pandora's colour deepened. 'Do they think we're having problems?'

'Of course they do,' he said with a touch of irritation. 'They're not stupid. They can tell we're not talking to each other when they're not there.'

'So what are we going to do?'

'We can start by having dinner together,' he said. 'And talking.'

Nancy had left cold chicken and salad. By tacit agreement they ate it in the kitchen, perhaps hoping that the informal atmosphere would encourage conversation. They tried. They both tried, but every time they started talking they would find themselves wandering into dangerous areas that brought back Cindy or

Quentin or the times they had kissed and the words would fizzle out into yet another awkward silence.

This was hopeless, thought Pandora, miserably racking her brains for another impersonal topic of conversation. How could she sit here and talk when all she wanted to do was get up and walk round the table to put her arms around his neck and slide onto his lap, to bury her face in his throat and pretend that this was all just a horrible dream and that he wasn't going to go away and leave her here without him?

They ended up talking about soil erosion, which seemed to be the only subject without any fraught undercurrents. Pandora's understanding of soil erosion was limited, to say the least, but they persevered anyway, with her asking questions and Ran answering and neither of them listening to a word. All in all, they were both relieved when the meal was over and Ran suggested that they have their coffee outdoors.

It was easier in the dusky lavender light outside. Pandora sat on the terrace steps and cradled her hands around her mug, reassured by the twilight that blurred her face. The sky was a dark, smoky blue and the air was still and fragrant. Ran sat still and silent beside her, carefully apart but near enough for her to touch him if she reached out her hand.

The temptation to do just that was so strong that Pandora tightened her grip on the mug and reminded herself about Cindy. It was stupid to try and avoid the subject, she thought. Far better to get it out in the open. 'Did you get the message from Cindy?' she asked into the semi-darkness. See, it was easy when she tried. Hadn't her father always said that if you talked about the things you were afraid of they suddenly didn't seem so bad?

'Yes, I rang her when I got back.' There was a faint

note of strain in Ran's voice and Pandora glanced at him from under her lashes, but his expression was lost in the shadows.

'Is she coming over?' she made herself ask.

'I don't know.' Ran paused for so long that Pandora thought that he had finished, but he went on eventually, picking his words with care. 'She's just finished her contract, and when I left she was due to go back to the States on leave. We've been together some time and Cindy thought it was a good opportunity to "give each other some space", as she put it. Neither of us has ever wanted marriage and we've always made a point of keeping our independence, but this seemed the right time to go our separate ways for a while and to see whether we really do want to be together or not. With her experience, Cindy could easily get another job out in Mandibia, but she isn't in any hurry at the moment. We're just seeing how things go.'

Pandora's white shirt was a pale blur in the dusk. She couldn't imagine not wanting to be with Ran. 'Will you still go back to Africa even if she decides to stay in the States?'

'Of course.' He sounded surprised. 'I've got a job to do, and besides. . .' He paused and looked out across the dark summer garden. 'Africa is a very special place,' he said after a while. 'I would miss it if I didn't go back.'

'Don't you think you might miss England too?'

Ran turned to look at her through the dusk. Her dark eyes gleamed in the faintness of her face and, in the hush, the evening scent of stocks drifted up from the flowerbeds below. 'I'm beginning to think I might,' he said slowly.

There was another silence, but this time the awkwardness had gone, leaving behind a different kind of tension that coiled itself insidiously around them. Pandora put down her mug and the tiny chink it made against the stone seemed to reverberate through the night.

'Why does Africa mean so much to you?' she asked.

'It's a big place,' he said, remembering. 'The African sky is huge and the horizon goes on for ever. Things are on a bigger scale out there—the landscape, emotions, problems, *everything*. The colours are brighter, the smells more intense, the light sharper, and the streets are always full of people and music and noise.' He glanced at Pandora. 'You would love it.'

'I can't imagine ever going anywhere like that,' she said wistfully. 'It's different for you. You grew up there, didn't you?'

'In West Africa,' he said. 'My father was a doctor. He went out to run a remote clinic when I was four, and he never left. I can't really remember what life was like before Africa. I didn't come back to England until I was sent to boarding-school, kicking and screaming. I was used to running wild in the African bush, so you can imagine what a shock it was.'

'It sounds a very romantic childhood,' said Pandora enviously, thinking of her staid English upbringing.

'I wouldn't describe it quite like that,' said Ran, a thread of bitterness in his voice.

'But why? Weren't you happy?'

'Oh, I was all right, but my father wasn't. My mother left when I was five and he never got over it.'

Pandora stared at him, appalled. 'Your mother *left* you? How could she?'

'Quite easily, I gather.' His face was still hidden in the shadows. 'Having a baby was just a means to an end to her. When she first met my father, he was considered quite a catch—a Masterson of Kendrick

Hall and all that. She was, apparently, a beautiful girl, and my father fell head over heels in love with her. She had visions of herself queening it here, but she reckoned without his social conscience.'

Ran sat forward, resting his elbows on his thighs and linking his hands between his knees. 'My father loved Kendrick Hall, but he was always conscious of the privilege of growing up in a place like this, and he was determined to use his skills where they were most needed. As soon as I was old enough he accepted a post in a remote bush clinic in Ghana.

'My mother was horrified. She had assumed that a wife and child would be enough to ensure that he gave up what she called his "do-gooding ideas", but now she found herself dragged off to darkest Africa and left alone with a small boy while my father threw himself into his work. If she had been a different woman, she would have worked with him, but instead she complained about the heat and flies and the boredom. She wanted to give grand dinner parties and have people to stay for the weekend at Kendrick Hall, and when she realised that she wasn't going to get that kind of life from my father she left. And I was just five.'

Pandora's heart cracked at the thought of the bewildered little boy. 'But surely she didn't just leave you behind?'

Ran shrugged. 'She wasn't the maternal type. She'd only had me in an attempt to make my father stay at home, and that obviously hadn't worked. I would have been a permanent reminder of her failure.'

'I'm sorry,' said Pandora inadequately.

'Looking back, I think she was right to leave instead of wasting her life complaining,' he said. 'But at the time it tore my father apart. It was an early lesson for me on how destructive a marriage can be. Since then

I've seen too many couples shackled together in misery and frustration, just as my parents were, and I decided early on not to make the same mistake.'

She wanted to shout at him, to tell him that it didn't have to be like that, but she knew that he wouldn't listen. His mother's departure had scarred him deeper than he liked to think. 'Didn't your father ever try and persuade her to come back?'

'He wrote to her, but she never replied. I think she went to Australia in the end, but not until she'd been back to Kendrick Hall and told Eustace how cruel my father had been. He didn't believe in divorce, apparently, and he wrote to my father. I don't know what he said—my father burnt the letter—but the two of them never communicated again. That broke his heart all over again. He'd never got on all that well with Eustace, but he loved Kendrick Hall.'

Ran's voice was bleak with memory. 'He used to sit on the veranda on the hot African nights and tell me stories about growing up here. Africa was the only home I could remember, but my father's home was always here, in spite of the fact that he never saw it again.' He sighed. 'When I heard that I'd inherited Kendrick Hall, my first reaction was bitterness that it was too late for my father. He died only six months before Eustace.'

He fell silent, and Pandora sat pensively beside him, thinking about the bitterness Ran had grown up with. It wasn't surprising that he was against marriage after being abandoned like that. How different things would have been if his mother had stayed and helped build a life for them all together.

'What are you thinking about?' asked Ran after a while and she sighed.

'Oh. . .just how different my childhood was, growing

up in a happy family. We never had any money or went anywhere exciting, but that never mattered when we were children. We used to have a wonderful time playing together when we were smaller—and when we weren't fighting.'

Ran smiled. 'Are your brothers like you?'

'They take after Mum,' said Pandora, shaking her head. 'She's always been smart and practical, while Dad's hopelessly vague. I'm more like him,' she added in a burst of honesty and Ran's smile deepened.

'I thought you might be.'

'It's funny,' she went on without thinking. 'Mum and Dad are as different as can be, and yet somehow they're perfect together. Still, they say opposites attract, don't they?' Too late, she heard her own words echo into the silence and realised that they could apply equally well to her and Ran. 'I mean. . .not always, of course,' she stammered.

Ran was watching her averted profile. 'I always used to think it was rather a dubious theory,' he said. 'But I think I'm beginning to change my mind.'

Pandora turned her head at that and they looked at each other through the deepening dusk. Very slowly, Ran reached out to brush aside her hair and rest his hand at the nape of her neck so that his thumb could caress the smooth line of her jaw. His touch was tantalisingly light—just enough to snarl every nerve in her body with desire—and when the pressure of his hand increased to slide her along the step towards him she didn't even think of resisting.

The furious tension of the last few days was forgotten, the future too remote to think about. Nothing mattered but this moment in the soft blue hush, with his hand beneath her hair and his body only inches away.

Instinctively, Pandora leant towards him. . .just as a horn blared at the front of the house and car wheels scrunched on the gravel. Inside, Homer began a noisy welcome.

Myra and Elaine were back.

CHAPTER NINE

'ONLY two more days!' Myra sighed to Pandora the next morning as they sat round the breakfast table. 'Just today and tomorrow and then it's your exhibition. We've enjoyed ourselves so much, but after that we really will have to go. We've stayed far too long as it is.'

'Not at all,' said Ran. 'But if you do have to go we should give you a proper farewell and celebrate your last day here.'

Pandora thought that he alone would want to celebrate the Americans' departure, but she smiled brightly. 'Yes, let's do something together,' she suggested. 'I'll have to go into the gallery early on Friday, but why don't we take a picnic down to the river tomorrow? If the weather stays like this it'll be as nice there as anywhere.'

Myra and Elaine were delighted with the idea and went happily off to Hadrian's Wall. Pandora gathered up the breakfast dishes and took them along to the kitchen. Ran had disappeared into the study to take a call from Mandibia, and she wasn't sorry that he was occupied with some problem that was brewing there.

They had been so close to kissing last night! The sound of the Americans' arrival had jerked them apart, and Ran had become instantly brisk as he'd gone in to greet them. It was impossible to tell whether he regretted their untimely return or not. In bed that night, he had been scrupulously careful not to touch her, and Pandora had begun to wonder whether she had imagined the pressure of his hand at the nape of her neck and the shivery caress of his thumb. Embarrassed, frustrated, horribly uncertain, she'd retreated once more behind a façade of stilted politeness.

There was no more to be done for the exhibition. Pandora felt at a loose end. It seemed a very long day. She took Homer for a long walk, drove into Wickworth to do some shopping for the picnic the next day and helped Nancy with the cooking, but none of it distracted her. 'Only two more days!' Myra's words pounded in her brain. In two more days it really would all be over, and this time it would be for good. Myra and Elaine would go back to the States, Ran would go back to Africa and she. . .well, she would go back to her pottery.

Ran seemed to spend the whole day on the phone. Pandora could hear his crisp voice sorting out what appeared to be a particularly intractable problem whenever she went through the hall. It was a timely reminder of how different his life was from hers, she thought. For a few brief weeks, their lives had converged, but in two days' time they would pass each other and carry on as before in opposite directions, never to meet again.

The knowledge filled Pandora with a sense of desperation. If two days was all she had left with Ran, she should make the most of them. That night, she lay in bed beside him and remembered what he had said that first night about not kissing her unless she asked. Could she? Did she dare? Rolling over, she stared at his back, rehearsing what she would say. Perhaps she didn't need to say anything. Perhaps all she needed to do was reach out and run her hand over his flank. His back was both tantalising and daunting. She willed him to turn, to show her that he wasn't asleep either, but he lay resolutely facing away, and in the end Pandora's courage failed her. With a sigh, she rolled back to stare at the window and wonder how bitterly she would regret her cowardice in the years to come.

They set off for the river just after eleven the next day. The heat was gathering into a thunderstorm somewhere behind the hills but for now the sky was blue and clear, and only the heaviness of the air gave any hint of what was to come. Overhung with willows and old oaks and scarcely more than a stream, the river meandered idyllically through the fields beyond the woods.

They spread the rugs in the grassy shade of an oak, where the river bent and rippled on its way. On the far side, fat cows were browsing knee-deep in buttercups, and Homer pricked up his ears, but Ran's stern, 'No,' was enough to make him flop down next to Pandora with a disappointed sigh. Pandora was determined not to waste the day regretting last night's indecision or agonising about the future. She was on sparkling form, and as Myra and Elaine were equally determined to enjoy themselves it was a high-spirited party. Ran himself was content to sit back and watch the three women indulgently, keeping an eagle eye on Homer at the same time.

Throughout the hot afternoon, they lay indolently on the rugs in the shade with a bottle of champagne. When the last drop had been finished and the last strawberry ceremoniously divided, Myra proposed a walk. Homer scrambled up at the magic word, but Pandora was too lazy to move, and in the end only Elaine had enough energy to go with them. The three of them disappeared round a bend in the river, leaving Ran and Pandora alone with the browsing cows and the still afternoon.

Ran stretched out on one of the rugs and closed his

eyes, linking his hands behind his head and wriggling his shoulders into a comfortable position. 'Those two have got more energy than is good for them!'

'They're nice, though, aren't they?' Pandora wrapped her arms around her knees. 'I think I'll miss them when they go.' She didn't tell Ran how much she would miss him.

'The Hall will certainly seem quieter without them,' Ran agreed lazily without opening his eyes.

Pandora lay back beside him, not touching him but content for now just to be near him. If she turned her head, she could let her eyes drift over his face and the lean, hard length of his body. He was so familiar that she couldn't imagine a time when she hadn't known the line of his nose and jaw, the cool mouth and the warm hands and the whole still, quiet strength of him. How was she going to be able to say goodbye to him and walk out of his life?

Closing her eyes against the prospect, Pandora refused to let herself think beyond the here and now, the hot summer afternoon and the faint ripple of the stream and Ran utterly relaxed beside her.

Something was tickling her nose, enticing her out of sleep. Pandora mumbled and brushed at it, but it persisted and after a while she opened her eyes languidly. Ran was propped up on one elbow beside her, tickling her face with a piece of grass, his grey eyes warm and peculiarly intent.

'I must have dropped off,' she said, but she made no move to sit up. She wanted to lie there for ever, held by the look in his eyes and the hazy excitement of his body.

'You did more than drop off. You've been sound asleep for the last hour!' Ran's smile enveloped her, seeping through her skin to gather in a warm glow deep inside.

'Are the others back yet?'

'No, but I can hear their voices. They'll be here any minute.'

It was strange the way they could be having one conversation with their mouths and quite a different one with their eyes. Ran tossed his piece of grass aside and leant over Pandora on the pretext of brushing a fly from her hair, but his hand stayed there, twisting the dark strands around his fingers.

Pandora couldn't have moved if she had tried. The air between them was tightening, tightening, shortening the gap between them, pulling them together with an almost irresistible force. Ran was going to kiss her at last. Any moment now his body would come down on hers, and his lips would be warm and sure and possessive. Pandora had no thought of resisting. Why should she resist something that was so inevitable and so *right*?

Her hands lifted to his shoulders and she smiled, and his face changed. 'Pandora, he began urgently. 'Do you remember—?'

She never heard the rest of the question. A shaggy nose was thrust suddenly between them and a wet tongue began licking her face with exuberant affection. 'Homer!' Half laughing, half ready to weep with frustration, Pandora rolled away from him, fending him off with her hands. 'Stop it!'

Ran pulled Homer back so that she could sit up. 'Immaculate timing as ever, Homer!' he said resignedly.

Homer sat with his tongue lolling out and looked so pleased with himself that Pandora couldn't help laughing. A second later, he had bounded off again to welcome Myra and Elaine who were hurrying around the bend in the river. 'Perhaps it's just as well Homer interrupted us when he did,' said Ran, helping Pandora to her feet. He didn't let go of her hand immediately, but stood looking down at her.

She glanced up into his smiling eyes and then at the Americans who were almost upon them. 'Perhaps,' she agreed reluctantly, and his fingers tightened around hers.

'Sorry we were so long!' Myra panted up to them, fanning herself with her hat. 'Have you been bored waiting for us?'

Ran let go of Pandora's hand. 'No,' he said. 'We haven't been in the least bored, have we, Pandora?'

She could never be bored when she was with him. 'No,' said Pandora softly.

'We thought we'd better head back,' Elaine puffed, and pointed at the sky behind them. 'It's going to pour any minute now.'

Even as she spoke, there was a rumble of thunder. Ran and Pandora turned to see a black mass of clouds advancing menacingly to blot out the sun. Galvanised out of the dream-like bubble that had enclosed them, they shoved a rug each into the Americans' arms, grabbed the baskets and ran. The first splattering raindrops hit them just as they reached the woods, and they were all drenched by the time they made it back to the house. 'It wouldn't have been a real English picnic unless it had rained,' Pandora assured them breathlessly as they stumbled into the shelter of the Hall.

Dinner was a gay affair that night, and they were all laughing as they said goodnight as usual on the landing. Later, Pandora would wish she could remember what amused them so much, why she and Ran were still laughing helplessly as they fell back together against the bedroom door, closing it behind them, but the joke, if a joke it had been, was forgotten as soon as they looked into each other's eyes.

The laughter tailed off and their smiles faded slowly as something new and scary in its intensity leapt into life between them. Ran levered himself away from her, but he didn't step back. For a long, long moment they just stared at each other while all pretence dropped away and they faced the truth that could be denied no longer.

'I wanted to kiss you down by the river,' said Ran at last. His voice was very deep and very low and Pandora felt it vibrating through her.

Her senses were fluttering just beneath her skin. 'I know,' she whispered.

'Would you have minded if I had?'

She shook her head, her eyes still held by his. 'No.'

Ran reached out a gentle hand and smoothed the silky hair back from Pandora's face, letting his fingers slide caressingly over her cheek. 'I was going to ask you if you remembered what I promised.'

'You said you wouldn't touch me again unless I asked.'

'So you do remember!' A smile glimmered in his eyes. 'I'd like to kiss you again now,' he said softly. 'But I won't unless you ask me.'

Pandora was strumming with anticipation. Slowly, unsmilingly, she began to undo the buttons of his shirt one by one. Ran didn't say anything, but he stood very still as she tugged the shirt free of his trousers at last and lifted her hands to his broad, bare chest, spreading them luxuriously over his skin and trailing them down to the arrowing V of dark hairs before sliding them teasingly around to his sides.

'Pandora...' warned Ran with a groan, and she smiled at last, lifting her face to his.

'Would you kiss me, Ran? Please?'

He bent his head until his lips were almost touching hers. 'Now let's see how *you* like being kept waiting,' he murmured, teasing, changing his mind at the last minute and kissing her earlobe instead. His mouth pressed, warm and tantalising, to the soft skin at the angle of her jaw and throat and Pandora arched her head back with a murmur that was part protest, part pleasure as he planted kisses along her jawline and around to the other ear before drifting down her throat.

She was wearing an Indian skirt with a cotton camisole top. Ran's fingers were deft, far steadier than hers had been as he undid the camisole and slid it off her shoulders, then bent to continue the devastating trail of his kisses, along her arms, over her breasts, his hands cupping and curving a burning path for his lips to follow.

'Ran!' Afire with desire, Pandora gasped his name and twisted her fingers pleadingly in his hair until she felt him smile against her breast.

'Well?' he murmured into her throat, letting his mouth travel upwards.

Pandora slid her arms around his neck as he lifted his head. 'Kiss me,' she whispered. She was still leaning against the door, her eyes huge and dark with longing. 'Please kiss me. Kiss me the way you wanted to kiss me by the river.'

'I'll show you how I wanted to kiss you.' There was a ragged edge to Ran's voice as he lifted her high in his arms and carried her over to the bed. Another time, he had dumped her down in exasperation; now he laid her down as if she was a precious gift. 'Your hair was all tumbled, like this,' he said, spreading her hair over the pillow, rubbing its softness through his fingers. 'And then you woke up and smiled at me,' he went on slowly, 'and I wanted to do this. . .'

He bent just as before, and just as before Pandora's hands slid to his shoulders, but this time there was no Homer to shove his head between them, no voices approaching, nothing to stop their lips meeting in a kiss of inexpressible sweetness. Pandora sank into it with a murmured sigh of release, letting her hands drift over the sleek, steely strength of his shoulders, loving the feel of his muscles flexing beneath her fingers.

The kiss went on and on, until they were both intoxicated with its piercing pleasure, touching and tasting and laughing shakily at its unexpected power. 'Now you know how I was going to kiss you if that dog of yours hadn't interfered,' said Ran a little unsteadily. 'And you know why it was just as well he did, or I wouldn't have been able to stop when our guests appeared, and we would all have got even wetter than we did.'

'What would you have done?' murmured Pandora mischievously, kissing his ear, his jaw, his throat.

'I would have peeled off your clothes,' he said, his voice deep and warm as he suited actions to words, 'and then I would have taken off mine, and *then* I would have lain down beside you in the shade, like this.' He lowered himself gently onto Pandora, bracing himself so that their bodies were just touching, and she shivered at the thrill of his skin on hers, his warmth and his hardness.

She trailed her fingers down his arms. 'It's lucky Homer was there,' she teased.

'I didn't feel very lucky at the time,' said Ran with feeling.

Pandora quivered with laughter and slid her hands up his flanks. 'How do you feel now?'

'I feel like doing this,' he murmured against her lips, and kissed her again.

Her skin was pearly, coolly luminous in the moonlight, but Pandora felt as if she was burning with the desire that ran molten along her veins. Ran's hands were very sure as they slid possessively over her, exploring her supple, satiny warmth with increasing urgency. She dissolved beneath his touch, drowned in the indescribable delight of his lips drifting over her skin. All that was left was the insistent throb of need, and she called his name beseechingly, afraid of the wild, unstoppable sweep of excitement that was carrying her into unknown territory.

And then she was no longer afraid, because Ran was with her and within her, holding her tight as the rush of sensations threatened to overwhelm her. 'Pandora!' His voice didn't sound like him at all. Pandora ran her hands over his firm body with a sort of desperation, wanting him closer, deeper, wanting all of him. He was the only reality in a world that had spun into touch and taste and the urgent rhythm of desire. She hadn't known that it was possible to *feel* like this.

Then the rhythm changed and the whirling, swirling rush converged into one desperate need that bound them together and arrowed them at last into an explosion of glorious release that caught Pandora quite unprepared. Stunned, overawed, she could only cling to him during that one timeless, eternal moment when everything stopped.

Gradually, very gradually, her senses returned, swimming back through the euphoria. Ran was lying heavily on top of her, his face pressed into her throat, and he was breathing jerkily. Pandora had forgotten to breathe

at all. She took an experimental breath and eased the
fingers that were digging into his shoulders, smoothing
her hands lovingly over his back instead and kissing his
hair.

Ran stirred. He kissed her throat and rolled over
onto his side, taking Pandora with him so that they
were facing each other. He brushed the hair away from
her face with tender hands, kissing her eyes, her mouth.
'I feel lucky now,' he said.

'So do I,' said Pandora, tears of happiness stinging
her eyes. There was no one to hear, but they were
whispering, reluctant to shatter the golden enchant-
ment that still enveloped them. 'Very lucky.'

He held her in his arms then, stroking her hair
rhythmically and smoothing his other hand over her
skin as if to reassure himself that she was real. They
had no need of words. Pandora rested her head against
his chest and listened to his heart slowly thudding. She
felt safe and cherished, filled with a boundless wonder
at the rapture she and Ran had shared.

The wonder was still with her when Ran woke her
with kisses early the next morning. Pandora stretched
sleepily beneath his possessively drifting hands. 'Is it
time to get up?'

'No,' said Ran, mumbling kisses along her shoulder.
'You can go back to sleep if you want to.'

Pandora smiled as joy shivered down her spine. She
arched her body at his touch and wrapped her arms
around his neck. 'And if I don't want to?'

Ran lifted his head and looked down into her face
with an answering smile. Pandora wondered how she
could ever have thought his eyes cold as he lowered his
mouth to hers. 'I'm sure we'll be able to think of
something to pass the time,' he said.

*   *   *

For Pandora, the day passed in a daze of happiness where considerations of past and future were pushed to the back of her mind. It was enough to be able to look at him and remember the breathless excitement caused by his hands gentling over her curves, and the glorious, gasping pleasure of his body.

At least, she thought it was. She thought it until five o'clock when she made her way down the stairs, tossing the keys to the van in her hand. The yellow dress had come back from the cleaners just in time, and she had put it on, ostensibly in honour of the exhibition, but really for Ran. She had already spent a couple of hours at the gallery that morning, helping Quentin get everything ready, but she still wanted to arrive early, so they had agreed that she would drive herself in and Ran would follow later with Elaine and Myra. In other circumstances, Pandora would have been jittery with nerves about her first exhibition, but today she couldn't think beyond the heart-stopping wonder of the night before and the joy of the night to come.

Intending to let Ran know that she was going, Pandora headed towards the study just as the phone rang. Ran must have been sitting right beside it, for he answered it before it had time to ring twice. 'Cindy!' Pandora heard him say, and she stopped dead outside the door, which stood just ajar. 'You're *where*?' he went on after a minute. 'When did you arrive?' There was a pause while he listened. 'So you've definitely decided to take the job? I see.' The keys were digging into Pandora's clenched hand as he paused again. 'I'm glad you're here, Cindy,' he said at last. 'I've been thinking about you a lot, and I need to talk to you too, but you're right, we can't really discuss it on the phone.'

For a while, all Pandora could hear was him saying yes occasionally as he listened to Cindy, but then he

spoke again. 'Tomorrow's a bit difficult.' He hesitated.
'Why don't you come up the day after, when I've got
rid of my guests? We'll be alone then, and we can talk
properly.'

Pandora didn't wait to hear any more. She walked
numbly out to her old van and started the engine.
Cindy had obviously made up her mind to go back to
Africa and be with Ran. He had said that it would be
easy for her to get a job and it seemed as if that was
what she had done.

And now she was coming here, as soon as he had
'got rid of' his guests. That presumably included her
since he was so anxious to be alone with Cindy.
Pandora was stricken, too desperate to cry or be angry.
It wasn't as if Ran had made any secret of his relationship with Cindy. He might have made love to her last
night, but he had never said that he loved her, or made
any promises about the future. He was going to do just
what he had always said he would do: he was going
back to Africa and Cindy, and that would be that.

Pandora had no idea how she got to Wickworth.
There was a suffocating band of misery around her
heart, but somehow she managed to pin a smile to her
face and pretend to be normal as she stood with
Quentin in the gallery and greeted people as they
arrived. The exhibition was a tremendous success;
everyone told her so. Pandora watched the little red
'sold' stickers appearing like measles and wondered
how they could bring her so little pleasure. Quentin
had invited all the Wickworth bigwigs, and they filled
the gallery, drinking white wine and shouting at each
other over the hubbub.

Ran arrived a little later with Myra and Elaine in
tow. He was looking preoccupied, but he smiled when
he saw Pandora and fought his way through the crowd

towards her. 'I didn't get a chance to wish you luck,' he said. 'Why didn't you tell me you were going?'

'You were on the phone.' Pandora's mouth felt stiff and her head ached with the strain of appearing normal. Would he tell her about Cindy, or would he keep that particular piece of news to himself?

'You could have put your head round the door.' Ran frowned as he looked at her, and she knew that he had seen the strain in her eyes. 'What's the matter?'

'Nothing,' she said flatly. If he didn't want to tell her, he didn't. What could he tell her that she didn't already know anyway? 'It's just rather stuffy in here.' Conscious of a terrible tightness in her throat, she was suddenly desperate to get away before she cried. 'Excuse me, I must just have a word with Quentin.'

She could feel his eyes on her all evening as she smiled and chatted feverishly. Thanks to Myra and Elaine, who sang their praises enthusiastically, everyone soon knew that she and Ran were supposedly married, and once they realised who Ran was, they were inundated with dinner invitations which they had to fend off with vague replies.

It was the longest evening of Pandora's life. She stuck by Quentin's side and Ran's smile began to look as strained as hers, but he made no effort to take her aside and explain about Cindy. He could have said *something*, Pandora thought desperately. Or was she just expected to keep her part of the bargain and leave as soon as Myra and Elaine had gone? If that was what he wanted, that was what she would do. He needn't think that he was going to have any trouble getting rid of *her* before his precious Cindy arrived!

At last the gallery began to empty, but it still wasn't over. 'Myra and I would like to take you and Ran out to dinner,' said Elaine, beckoning Pandora over to where they stood with Ran. It was the nearest Pandora had been to him all evening, but she deliberately didn't look at him. 'It's our way of thanking you both for all you've done for us, and, of course, of celebrating your success!'

Pandora had never felt less like celebrating, but anything would be better than going home and being alone with Ran, knowing that he would be waiting for a good moment to tell her about Cindy. 'That's very sweet of you,' she said. 'But if we're going to celebrate do you mind if we include Quentin? If it wasn't for him, I wouldn't have had the exhibition at all, and he's been marvellous. He's the one who's got me through the last few weeks.' Out of the corner of her eye, she saw Ran's face tighten, and looked quickly away.

'Of course we don't mind,' said Myra. 'He must come too. We'll have a party!'

Pandora thought that the dinner would never end. Desperate not to let Ran know how close to tears she was, she kept up a flow of brittle conversation and flirted feverishly with Quentin, who was clearly puzzled but obliging. Myra and Elaine didn't seem to notice anything amiss. They were more delighted with Pandora's success than she was and kept telling Ran how proud he should be of her.

Ran didn't look proud. He looked grim and withdrawn, but was making a heroic effort to behave normally. Pandora insisted on sitting next to Quentin, and avoided his eye. She couldn't wait for this ghastly evening to be over, but dreaded the moment when it would be impossible to avoid being alone with him any longer.

At least she was spared the drive home. 'I'll need to take the van home,' she said to Myra as they came out of the restaurant. 'You and Elaine go back with Ran. and I'll follow you. I'm sure Quentin will walk me back to the van, won't you, Quentin?'

'Of course,' he said with alacrity, and Pandora took his arm and looked directly at Ran for the first time that evening.

'I'll see you later.'

She drove home as slowly as possible, hoping that Ran would have given up and gone to sleep, but he was waiting up for her, still fully dressed, his face set.

'I see you managed to drag yourself away from Quentin,' he said harshly as she shut the bedroom door behind her.

'Yes.' Pandora sat down at the dressing table and concentrated on brushing her hair so that she didn't have to face Ran directly.

'You must be very pleased with yourself,' Ran went on in the same hard voice. 'Two successful seductions and a successful exhibition in two days!'

'Yes, the exhibition went better than I expected,' said Pandora, ignoring the first part of his sentence. Her own voice sounded tight, and her throat ached with the effort of not crying. Why were they talking to each other like hostile strangers when this time last night he had carried her over to the big bed and laid her down and loved her? 'It was probably a mistake for you to come, though.'

'Why? My presence didn't stop you crawling all over Quentin Moss, which was obviously all you wanted to do!' Ran's tone was so savage that Pandora winced, but she managed to keep her voice cool.

'Actually, I was thinking of all those dinner invitations. How are you going to explain to all those people that I'm not in fact your wife?'

'How am *I* going to explain?'

'It was your idea,' she pointed out. 'I only agreed to pretend until Myra and Elaine left, and that's tomorrow. It's your problem after that—I'll be moving back to the stables as soon as they've gone.'

'I hope you're going to take that bloody dog with you!' said Ran cruelly.

'Of course,' she said, astonished at how calm she could sound when her heart was cracking, breaking, splintering into a thousand pieces just as the vase had done when it had smashed against the floor. 'After all, I've more than paid for the damage he did.'

Ran's jaw worked convulsively. 'I hadn't realised you were chalking everything up against your account.'

'No, you were the one who did that,' said Pandora bitterly, thinking of how he had used her.

There was a tense silence. 'Are you going to tell me what's wrong?' he said at last. The words sounded as if they had been forced out of him.

'No.'

'Does that mean that you're going to pretend that nothing's wrong?'

Pandora kept dragging the brush through her hair. If he had told her about Cindy himself, she might have told him, but he hadn't said anything. If he wanted to keep Cindy's imminent arrival a secret, fine, but he needn't think she was going to make a fool of herself by telling him that her world had fallen apart because she had stood outside the study door and overheard his conversation.

'No,' she said again, and looked away from his angry eyes in the mirror. She put down the brush. 'What are you going to say when all those dinner invitations start coming in for Mr and Mrs Masterson?' she asked flatly.

'I won't have to say anything.' Ran's face looked as if it had been carved from granite, and she had to clamp down on the sudden searing vision of him as he had been last night, smiling against her skin. 'Now that Elaine and Myra have agreed to send their clients to Kendrick Hall, the builders can get on with the renovations, and I'll be leaving for Africa as soon as they start.'

'That's all very well for you, but what about me? I've got to stay here. What happens when I meet them in Wickworth?'

He shrugged callously. 'Tell them that you've left me for Quentin, or, if you'd rather portray yourself as the injured party, you can always say that I've left you and that you've moved to the stables because Kendrick Hall had too many memories.'

Did he really think that memories could be left behind that easily? He was part of her now, whatever happened. Wherever she went in the future, the memory of Ran and his smile and his hard, exciting body would go with her, and she was just going to have to learn to live with it.

'And in the meantime?' she asked. 'I presume you won't be able to leave immediately?'

He could have told her about Cindy then, but he didn't. Instead he picked up a pillow from the bed. 'In the meantime, I suggest you stay away from Wickworth. It shouldn't be for long.' He looked at Pandora still sitting at the dressing table and his expression was bleak and bitter. 'You can have the bed tonight,' he said. 'I'm going to sleep on the sofa.'

CHAPTER TEN

PANDORA watched Myra and Elaine's car slow down at the end of the drive, pause at the great stone gates and then, with a toot of the horn and a wave of an arm, turn out and disappear from sight.

She had been holding Homer's collar to stop him running after the car. Now she bent and clipped on his lead and handed it to Ran. 'Could you hold him while I go and get my things?'

She had already packed her bags and all she had to do was collect the dog bowl from the kitchen. When she went out again, Ran was stroking Homer's ears, but his hand stilled as he heard her feet crunch across the gravel and he straightened. He looked at the bags and the bowl in her other hand.

'So you're going?'

'I understood I'd paid my debt. I don't owe you anything more, do I?' Pandora deliberately kept her voice hard, and his mouth tightened.

'No, you don't owe me anything.'

Putting down the bags, she tucked the bowl under one arm so that she could tug off the rings he had given her. She held them out to him. 'You'd better have these back,' she said. 'You never know when you're going to need another wife.'

Almost reluctantly, Ran held out his hand and she dropped the rings into his palm without touching him. 'Goodbye,' she said, just as she'd practised it all night: coolly, impersonally, uncaringly.

His fingers closed convulsively over the rings. There

was a rigid, angry look to his jaw and his brows were
drawn together over his nose as he stared at her, as if
he couldn't quite believe what she was saying. For a
heart-lurching moment, Pandora thought that he might
be going to protest, but in the end he only said goodbye
in a flat voice and gave her back the end of Homer's
lead.

Furious with herself for that brief second of hope,
Pandora turned away without another word. Had she
really thought that he would ask her to stay when he
had Cindy arriving tomorrow? Bending to pick up her
bags, she set off up the drive towards the fork which
led to the stables, hampered by Homer, who had sensed
that something was very wrong and kept whining and
straining back to Ran.

'Come *on*, Homer,' she begged tearfully, hauling on
his lead. She wouldn't let herself cry until they reached
the stables, but as soon as the kitchen door closed
behind her she collapsed at the table and buried her
head in her arms. Distressed by her distraught sobs,
Homer whined and pushed his nose under her arm,
forcing his front paws onto her lap so that he could
stand and lick her face comfortingly. 'Oh, Homer, what
am I going to do?' wept Pandora, and buried her face
in his shaggy coat.

After a sleepless night, she made herself go into the
studio early the next morning. This was her life now,
and she had better get on with it. She had lived happily
without Ran before, and she would live happily without
him again.

One day.

One day this black misery would ease and she would
smile again. One day. . .but not yet.

Pandora kneaded the clay mindlessly while the tears
rolled slowly down her cheeks. By the end of the

afternoon, she hadn't managed to do anything except watch the wheel turning endlessly, as empty and useless as her life without Ran. It should have been raining to match her mood, but instead the golden afternoon light was pouring across the courtyard, reminding her of the day she had lain by the river with Ran.

She got up abruptly to banish the memories. She must stop crying like this! Desperate to think of something else—anything else—Pandora went outside and sat down on the mounting block, willing herself not to remember how Ran had stood there and brushed his fingers through her hair. Closing her eyes, she leant back against the wall and tried to blank her mind to everything except the droning bees and the feel of the sunlight on her face.

It worked. . .almost. Soothed by the peace, her slender body relaxed slowly, but as soon as she dropped the strict guard on her mind Ran's image shimmered back behind her eyelids. She could picture him so clearly: the watchful grey eyes, the distinct features, his cheek, his jaw, his mouth, the very texture of his skin.

Pandora's eyes snapped open, just in time to see Homer nose open the gate. 'Homer! Come here!' she called frantically, but it was too late. He was already trotting back towards the house that he had learnt to consider home.

Grabbing the lead, Pandora followed him, hoping that he would be diverted by some smell before he got to the Hall, but as she ran down the drive she saw that Homer had already found the man he was looking for.

Ran was just closing the door of his car. A tall, blonde girl stood next to him on the gravel, looking surprised at the sudden appearance of a huge, shambolic dog who was ecstatically greeting Ran like a long-lost master.

Pandora skidded to a halt, but they had seen her, and it was too late to turn round and run back. Drawing a deep, steadying breath, she walked down to join them. She was probably going to have to face Ran some time; it might as well be now, she thought. Ran had Homer under control by the time she reached them, and he handed him over to her as she came up. He was looking tired and tense, and there was a taut look about his mouth.

'I'm sorry,' she muttered, while every nerve strained to throw herself into his arms. 'He got out before I could stop him.'

Ran nodded. They looked at each other and then away. Cindy was eyeing them curiously. Catching her enquiring glance, Ran introduced Pandora reluctantly. 'This is Pandora Greenwood,' he said, carefully expressionless.

'Hi, I'm Cindy.' She smiled at Pandora in a friendly way. 'Do you live round here?'

'In the stables,' said Pandora, getting the words out with an effort. Cindy had a glowing, healthy look and a wide, open smile showing perfect teeth.

'Really?' said Cindy with interest. 'You didn't tell me you had any neighbours, Ran. I thought you were stuck out in the middle of nowhere on your own.' She turned back to Pandora. 'Is this your dog?' she asked, looking down at Homer with some amusement.

'Yes.' Pandora's lips felt stiff and her mouth didn't seem to work properly. She was very conscious of Ran standing next to Cindy. Obviously he hadn't found her worth mentioning, and a few last shreds of pride helped her pull herself together. 'He's very naughty, I'm afraid.'

'I think he looks cute.' Cindy ruffled Homer's head. 'What a great place to have a dog! I had no idea it

would be so beautiful up here. It must be wonderful
living somewhere like this.'

It had been until yesterday. 'Yes,' said Pandora
again. She bent to clip on Homer's lead and managed
a smile as she straightened. 'Enjoy your stay.' She
glanced at Ran's shoulder, unable to look him in the
eye. 'I'll try and keep Homer out of your way.'

She would keep herself out of the way too, she added
silently as she walked away.

Pandora lay on her bed fully clothed that night and
stared at the ceiling, hugging Homer to her. Ran would
have said that she shouldn't let him on the bed.

Ran... Every time she thought of him, she flinched
at the rawness of his absence. She wished she hadn't
met Cindy. Just knowing of her existence had been bad
enough, but seeing her had only served to convince her
that loving Ran was hopeless. If only Cindy hadn't
been so obviously nice. If she had been horribly unsuitable for him, there might—just *might*—have been a
chance that he would realise it when he saw her again;
but she wasn't. She was just what Ran had said she
was: bright and pretty and confidently capable. Exactly
the kind of woman he needed with him in Africa.

Pandora tortured herself imagining Ran and Cindy
together. Cindy had been so natural with him that even
if she hadn't known she would have guessed that they
had been lovers. Were they lovers again tonight? Was
Cindy lying in the wide bed running her hands over
Ran's body and gasping at the excitement of his touch?
The pain was so sharp at the thought that Pandora had
to bite down hard on her lip to stop herself crying out.

By the morning she had come to a decision. She
couldn't bear to be near Ran knowing that Cindy was
with him. It was time to accept that she had never been

more than a means to an end for him. Packing her bag, Pandora put Homer in the van and shut up the stables. She had no idea where she was going. All she knew was that she had to get away.

She drove to Wickworth first. Quentin had given her her first exhibition and he still had a gallery full of her pottery. She owed it to him to let him know that she was going. Parking the van, she walked down towards the gallery and past the flower stall where Ran had bought her the yellow roses. It seemed an eternity ago.

A familiar car approached just as Pandora was waiting in a group to cross the road at the lights, and her heart lurched. Shrinking behind a bulky woman who was complaining about her varicose veins, she watched as the car went past. Ran and Cindy were laughing together, looking relieved and happy, and neither noticed Pandora standing stricken by the side of the road.

'I'm going away,' she told Quentin baldly when she reached the gallery.

He was setting an oil painting on an easel in the front window, but he put it down when he saw Pandora's face. 'Going away? Why, what on earth's happened?'

'I just need to get away for a while.'

'Have you had an argument with Ran?'

Even his name was enough to make her flinch. She nodded dumbly and Quentin looked concerned. 'I can't say that I ever took to him myself, but you should try and work things out with him. He is your husband after all.'

'He's not my husband.' Pandora gave a defeated little sigh. 'I'm sorry we lied to you, Quentin, but we were just pretending.'

'Ran wasn't pretending when he found me holding

your hands,' said Quentin drily. 'No one could fake that look of murderous rage.'

'We were just trying to convince Myra and Elaine that we were married, but we aren't. . .' Pandora's voice cracked and she put a hand up to her mouth to stop it trembling but it was too late.

'Hey. . .' Quentin put his arms around her and let her cry. 'So what if you aren't actually married? Any fool could see that you are in love with each other. . . even me.'

'Ran doesn't love me,' she sobbed against his shoulder. 'He couldn't wait to get rid of me so his girlfriend could come, and now she's here and they look so happy together. . .' She trailed off hopelessly, dissolving into fresh tears.

'Come on,' said Quentin with decision. 'Everyone can see you here in the window. I'll make you a cup of tea in the back and you can tell me all about it.'

It took some time for him to unravel the whole story. When she had finished, he smiled ruefully and told Pandora that she was mad to even think about leaving. 'Believe me, I wish I could think there might be a chance for me in all of this, but there isn't. I don't know what this Cindy is doing here, but it doesn't sound to me as if Ran is in love with her at all. You really should stay and talk to him.'

'No, I've got to go,' Pandora insisted, scrubbing her face wearily with the handkerchief he had lent her, and in the end Quentin sighed and promised that he would let her know when Ran had left so that she could come back.

'Where will you be?'

'I'm not sure.' Pandora drew a shuddering breath. 'Probably with my parents.' She hadn't thought beyond getting away, but now she wondered what they would think if she went running back to them. 'I don't know. . .I'll ring you.'

'Make sure you do,' said Quentin with mock sternness. 'Quite apart from anything else, I've already had a lot of enquiries about you as a result of the exhibition, so you may be getting some orders.' He hugged her goodbye at the door. 'Come back soon.'

Her parents welcomed her home without question. Pandora told them that she had just felt like a break and her mother, after one look at her face, refrained from asking what had happened. At least Homer was happy. He found an instant friend in her parents' Labrador and the two dogs spent their time rough and tumbling in the back garden. Pandora wished that she could adjust that easily. Sometimes she wanted Ran so badly that she found it hard to breathe. Racked by a terrible longing just to see him again, she felt as if she was suffocating in despair.

One day passed, then another, and another, and still it got no easier. Was this what it was going to be like for the rest of her life? Pandora sat at the kitchen table on the fourth day and looked down at her left hand, thinking how bare it looked without Ran's rings. The hot, sunny spell had left her skin lightly tanned and there was still a faint white band where the rings had been. She had got used to their heaviness and the flash and sparkle of the diamonds in the sun and now her hand felt curiously weightless and clumsy without them.

Her mother set a pot of tea on the table and poured out two cups. 'You haven't said much about having your exhibition,' she said carefully. 'Wasn't it a success?'

'Yes, yes, it was.' Pandora forced herself to sound

enthusiastic but it didn't really work. 'I sold almost everything. Quentin was delighted.'

'Quentin being the owner of the gallery? What's he like?'

She sipped her tea. 'He's very nice. Much nicer than I thought he was at first,' she said, and her mother looked at her thoughtfully.

'So he's not the man you're breaking your heart for?'

The cup rattled in the saucer as Pandora put it down unsteadily. She might have known she couldn't fool her mother. She had always been able to see right through her, just as Ran had, and she had a sudden agonising vision of Ran looking down at her with that exasperated look of his, Ran laughing as they fell back against the bedroom door, Ran smiling as he bent to kiss her. She looked back at her mother with anguished violet eyes. 'No,' she said despairingly. 'It's not Quentin.'

'Then who is it?'

Before Pandora could answer, Homer scrambled up from beneath the table where he and the Labrador had been taking a nap and gave a short bark of excitement. Ears pricked, he stood at the kitchen door, his tail waving from side to side, slowly at first and then with gathering speed.

'What's the matter with you?' asked Pandora's mother as she let him out, and Homer rushed to the front door, yelping excitedly. The next moment the doorbell pealed and he went wild, joined belatedly by the Labrador.

'I'd better go and see who it is,' sighed her mother. 'It's probably the verger for your father.'

She closed the door behind her, leaving Pandora numbly sipping her tea. Wrapped up in bitter-sweet memories, she was scarcely aware of the hubbub in the hall. Homer was completely over-excited about something. but it wasn't until a familiar voice ordered, 'Quiet!' that Pandora registered who the visitor was. She froze with her cup halfway to her mouth.

'Settle down, Homer,' said the voice, and Homer's barks obediently subsided to strangled moans of pleasure while the Labrador continued to bark jealously until shushed by her mother.

Hardly daring to believe what she had heard, Pandora put her cup very carefully down on its saucer. She didn't dare move for fear that it would all turn out to be a dream.

There was a murmur of voices outside and then the door opened. 'Is this the man you've been waiting for?' asked her mother, and stood aside to reveal Ran with a hard, anxious look on his face.

Pandora pushed back her chair and stood up, and the expression in her eyes told her mother everything she needed to know. 'It looks as if you are,' she said drily to Ran, and withdrew, quietly closing the door behind her.

There was utter silence as Ran and Pandora just looked at each other. Oblivious to the atmosphere, Homer rushed up to Pandora, wanting her to share his excitement at having found Ran again, and then back to Ran to reassure himself that he was still there. Pandora didn't even notice. She was still dazed by the wave of sheer joy that had slammed into her when she'd seen that it really was Ran, that he was here, that he was real.

It was Ran who spoke first. 'It's taken me four days to find you,' he said, and she hardly recognised his voice. 'Why did you leave like that? You didn't even say goodbye.'

'I couldn't,' she said unevenly.

'But you must have known how I'd feel when I found

out that you'd gone!' Ran was still standing by the door, as if ready to leave.

'I thought you'd be pleased.'

'*Pleased?*' he echoed incredulously. 'I've just spent the last four days in hell and you thought that I'd be pleased?'

Bewildered, Pandora made a helpless gesture. 'You were happy with Cindy.'

'I haven't been happy since that damned exhibition,' said Ran slowly. 'It was as if you'd withdrawn behind an invisible wall and I couldn't reach you any more.' He looked across the room at Pandora, whose knees were so weak that she was holding onto the back of a chair for support. 'I'd only just discovered what true happiness was, Pandora, and you wiped it out at a stroke.'

'But you looked so happy when I saw you with Cindy in Wickworth,' she said in anguish. 'You didn't notice me, but I saw you drive past. You were *laughing* together. I thought you'd worked everything out.'

'We had,' said Ran, still making no move to come nearer. Disgusted with their lack of response, Homer had thrown himself down on the floor with a sigh. 'We'd worked out that we had just avoided the biggest mistake of our lives. If I hadn't inherited Kendrick Hall and Cindy hadn't gone home on leave we would have carried on as we were, and neither of us would have discovered what it meant to be really in love. Cindy met an old boyfriend when she went back to the States, and she realised that the real thing had been waiting for her at home all the time.' Ran paused. 'And I met you.'

'Me?' said Pandora huskily.

'You,' he confirmed, and a smile started at the back of his eyes. 'The most exasperating girl I've ever come across! You're the last kind of girl I expected to fall in love with, Pandora, but from the moment I walked out of my study and saw you standing in the hall I didn't stand a chance.'

Pandora's eyes were enormous. 'You're in love with *me*?' she said oddly, and Ran walked forward at last to take her hands.

'Desperately,' he said. His fingers were warm and strong and reassuringly real around hers. 'I tried not to be. I kept reminding myself of my parents' marriage, and how it was much more sensible to stay as independent and uncommitted as I'd been with Cindy, but it wasn't any good. Every time you looked at me with those beautiful eyes, every time you smiled, I fell deeper and deeper in love.'

'Why didn't you tell me?' asked Pandora, curling her fingers more tightly around his.

'I wasn't used to being in love,' he said seriously. 'It was uncharted territory for me, and at first I wasn't sure how far I wanted to go. I knew that if I got too involved with you an open relationship wouldn't be enough. That was obvious as soon as I saw you with Quentin—I wanted to punch him in the mouth just because you smiled at him. I didn't know how you felt. Whenever I touched you, I would be sure that you felt the same as I did, but then you seemed so keen on Quentin that I didn't know what to think. . .and I didn't like that feeling at all. I'd always been in control of my life before, but you turned everything upside down.'

Pandora could feel the black misery evaporating as a tiny trickle of incredulous hope seeped through her, gathering pace until she was awash with it. 'I was only trying to make you jealous.'

'Well, you succeeded!' said Ran with a rueful smile. 'When Elaine suggested meeting my wife, I could picture you so clearly that it was a shock. I'd only met you once, and not in the best of circumstances, and I'd certainly never thought about having a wife before, but suddenly I had this image of you that wouldn't go away.'

He paused and his clasp on her hands tightened. 'I told myself that the important thing was to get the house to pay for itself so that I could go back to Africa, but subconsciously I just wanted an excuse to see you again. The trouble was that the plan backfired on me. I knew that you were only with me because I'd blackmailed you into being there and I realised that I had put myself in an impossible position. I was furious for letting myself get tied up in knots like that, and I'm afraid I took it out on you.'

'So that's why you were so cross!' Pandora could feel a smile building in an unstoppable wave. 'I thought you just found me infuriating.'

'It was wanting to kiss you and knowing that I shouldn't take advantage of you that I really found infuriating,' said Ran. 'After that time in the kitchen, I knew I'd have to promise not to kiss you again unless you asked me.'

'And I did,' she reminded him softly, and the look in his eyes sent joy surging through her.

'Yes, you did,' he remembered.

Pandora couldn't hold back the smile any longer. 'Would you kiss me if I asked you again, Ran?'

'Yes,' he said, his own smile dawning slowly as if he could hardly believe what she was saying. 'Oh, yes, I would.'

'Then would you kiss me now, Ran? I don't think I can bear to wait any longer!'

Ran drew her towards him, and his hands slid up her arms and over her shoulders to brush wonderingly over her face. 'Pandora,' he said unsteadily. 'Pandora, I love you.'

'And I love you.' It was wonderful to be able to say it at last. Pandora smiled trustingly up into his eyes, and then the waiting was over and he was kissing her — deep, desperate kisses that released all the pent-up feelings of the last four days. Pandora dug her fingers into the hard strength of his body as she leant into him and kissed him back almost frantically.

'Pandora, Pandora. . .' Ran was kissing her eyes, her lips, her nose, her lips again. 'Do you know how hard it was to lie next to you night after night, knowing that you were just inches away in that damned nightdress and not being able to touch you?'

'I know,' she gasped, breathless under the delicious assault of his hands and his mouth. 'Oh, I know. I wanted you so much I didn't know what to do with myself.'

'Then why did it take you so long to ask?' He smiled into her throat.

She nibbled kisses along his jaw. 'I had to be sure you'd want me to. . .' she whispered, and he kissed her again.

There was an old armchair by the kitchen window and Ran sat down on it, pulling Pandora onto his lap. Linking her arms around his neck, she rested her cheek against his with a sigh of happiness. 'You must have known I was in love with you that night,' she said.

'I hoped you were,' he said, stroking her hair. 'By that stage I'd given up telling myself that I'd be better off alone, and I knew that you were all I'd ever want, but I thought it would be better to tell you how I felt once the exhibition opening was over and Elaine and Myra had left. There was so much to discuss — like whether you'd be willing to come back to Africa with me—but I obviously left it too late.' He put her away from him slightly so that he could look into her face. 'Why did you change so suddenly? When I got to the gallery, it was as if you were a completely different person.'

'I overheard you talking to Cindy when she phoned,' Pandora admitted, shamefaced. 'I heard you ask her whether she'd definitely accepted the job, and I thought that meant she had decided to go back and work in Mandibia with you.'

'So that's what it was!' Ran pulled her back against him. 'The job she's accepted is in the States, but when she rang she just said that she had taken a job and she really wanted to see me. When she arrived she said that I'd been sounding a bit odd on the phone, and she was afraid that I might be jealous, so she thought she owed it to me to come and tell me in person that she'd decided to marry Bob and stay in the States.'

'But you said that you'd been thinking about her and wanted to talk to her alone too!'

'I did. I felt that *I* owed it to *her* to tell her about you. I wanted her to know the truth. We'd been close in Mandibia and we'll always be friends, but we were so relieved when we discovered that we were both looking for the words to say the same thing.' He twisted Pandora's hair around his fingers. 'Why didn't you tell me what you'd heard?'

'Because *you* didn't tell *me*,' she said, her voice muffled against his shoulder. 'I thought it meant you wanted Cindy back after all and couldn't wait to get rid of me.'

'I didn't tell you because I could see that something was wrong and I didn't want to make things worse,' said Ran ruefully. 'I should have insisted that you tell me that night, but I was so hurt and angry and jealous of Quentin that I decided that the night before hadn't meant anything to you after all.'

Pandora kissed his ear. 'I tried not to let it mean anything. You'd made it very clear that you would never get married, and I knew you would be going back to Africa as soon as you could, so I thought it would be easier for both of us if I pretended that I wasn't in love with you.'

'I had a lot to say about marriage, didn't I?' said Ran, smoothing his hand enticingly over her thigh. 'But I've learnt that commitment isn't something that you can decide about. It just is. I'm committed to you whether you'll have me or not, and there's absolutely nothing I can do about it.' His smile twisted. 'It was rather ironic that the day I realised that freedom meant nothing without you and decided to ask you to marry me you ran away.' Memory made his eyes bleak. 'I can't tell you how I felt when I found out that you had gone.'

'I couldn't bear the thought of seeing you with Cindy,' Pandora explained. 'It was bad enough being near you and not being able to tell you how I felt, but when I met her and saw how nice she was I realised that it was hopeless. I couldn't imagine that you would ever want me when you could have her.'

'Cindy *is* nice,' said Ran. 'But she's not you. She doesn't drive me to distraction, but she doesn't light up my life just by being in it either. She doesn't look like you and she doesn't smile like you and she doesn't make my heart go bump every time she walks into the room.' Sliding his hand beneath Pandora's hair, he pulled her close until their lips were almost touching. 'Cindy may be a nice, sensible, intelligent girl,' he murmured against her mouth, 'but I don't love her. I love *you*.'

This time the desperate relief had faded and their kisses were deep and tender and sweet with promise. Pandora felt as if she was dissolving with sheer happiness. 'How did you find me?' she mumbled blissfully at last against Ran's ear.

'With great difficulty,' he said. 'I ended up telling Cindy all about you and she said that I should tell you exactly how I felt. I was going to go straight back and see you after I'd taken her to the station in Newcastle, but we had plenty of time to get there so we decided to stop for a coffee in Wickworth. Cindy hadn't seen anything after coming all that way and it seemed churlish to dump her at the station. Besides, I was so relieved that she didn't love me that I'd have done anything for her.'

He paused, still twining his fingers lovingly in Pandora's hair. 'We had to walk past the gallery to get to the café. I was telling Cindy about your exhibition and we looked in the window to see if any of your pieces were still there, but I didn't see any pottery. All I saw was you standing in Quentin's arms.' He buried his face abruptly in her hair. 'I didn't know that it was possible to feel like that, Pandora. It was as if all the lights had gone out. I kept swinging between murderous jealousy, black despair and a terrible knowledge of how empty my life would be without you.'

Lifting his head, he kissed her again—a hard, possessive kiss. 'As soon as I'd put Cindy on the train, I drove straight back to the gallery. I thought you might still be there, but Quentin told me you'd gone. I think I may have misjudged him,' he admitted with a wry grin. 'I was just about ready to strangle him with jealousy, but he told me not to be such a fool as it was perfectly obvious that you were in love with me, even if I didn't deserve it.'

'Did you believe him?'

'Eventually, when I'd calmed down a bit. I felt a bit better when he told me that you'd been as miserable as I was, but all he knew was that you'd mentioned going back to your parents. Apparently you'd been a bit vague and hadn't given him an address, so I had to try and track down the Williamses instead. I got their number in the States from the estate solicitor, but they were away, and I couldn't do anything until I'd spoken to them. Fortunately they knew your parents' address, otherwise I don't know what I'd have done.'

'They must have been surprised to hear from you,' said Pandora. 'You didn't tell them about Homer and the vase, did you?'

'No, I just told them that he'd brought us together, which I thought would be a tactful way of putting it. I also said I wanted to marry you and take you to Africa, and would it be all right if I asked your parents to look after Homer instead. Do you think they'll mind?'

Pandora shook her head. 'Homer's already made himself at home, and Mum will be much stricter with him than I've ever been.' Her smile faded and she sat back so that she could look seriously into his eyes. 'Ran, do you really want to marry me?'

'I really do,' he said. 'I got so used to the idea when you were with me that sometimes I forgot that we *weren't* married. When you gave me back my rings, I felt as if you'd hit me.' Reaching into his jacket pocket, he pulled out the diamond engagement ring, which glinted welcomingly in the sunlight. 'Will you take this back, Pandora, and wear it for real?'

'This time I'll keep it,' Pandora promised as he slid it onto her finger where it belonged, and she kissed him.

'We'll get married as soon as we can,' said Ran, 'and

once the builders have started I'll take you to Africa. I might even take you out to the bush—but *not* if you're going to insist on crystal glasses!'

'All right, but only if I can wear my hat to the wedding,' she teased, and he grinned.

'I wouldn't marry you in anything else!'

Pandora sighed happily. 'Won't it be wonderful not to pretend any more? Everything we made up for Myra and Elaine is turning out to be true.'

'Oh?' said Ran, with a smile that sent a shiver of sheer joy down her spine. 'What about those six children we told them we were planning to have?'

She leant forward to kiss him. 'They might take a bit longer,' she said, 'but I'm sure we can work on it.'

MILLS & BOON®

Three women make a pact to stay single,
but one by one they fall, seduced by the
power of love!

Don't miss Penny Jordan's exciting new
miniseries—The Brides Bouquet coming to
you in the new Mills & Boon Presents line
in September 1996.

Look out for:

Woman to Wed? in September
Best Man to Wed? in October
Too Wise to Wed? in January '97

MILLS & BOON®

Weddings ✣ Glamour ✣ Family ✣ Heartbreak

Weddings By De Wilde

Since the turn of the century, the elegant and fashionable DeWilde stores have helped brides around the world realise the fantasy of their 'special day'.

Now the store and three generations of the DeWilde family are torn apart by the separation of Grace and Jeffrey DeWilde—and family members face new challenges and loves in this fast-paced, glamourous, internationally set series.

*For weddings, romance and glamour,
enter the world of*

Weddings By DeWilde

—a fantastic line up of 12 new stories from popular Mills & Boon authors

OCTOBER 1996

Bk. 1 SHATTERED VOWS - Jasmine Cresswell
Bk. 2 THE RELUCTANT BRIDE - Janis Flores

AND A SILVER PLATED PHOTO FRAME

FREE

Return this coupon and we'll send you 4 Mills & Boon Enchanted™ novels and a silver plated photo frame absolutely FREE! We'll even pay the postage and packing for you.

We're making you this offer to introduce you to the benefits of Reader Service: FREE home delivery of brand-new Mills & Boon Enchanted novels, at least a month before they are available in the shops, FREE gifts and a monthly Newsletter packed with information.

Accepting these FREE books and gift places you under no obligation to buy, you may cancel at any time, even after receiving just your free shipment. Simply complete the coupon below and send it to:

MILLS & BOON® READER SERVICE, FREEPOST, CROYDON, SURREY, CR9 3WZ.

No stamp needed

Yes, please send me 4 free Mills & Boon Enchanted novels and a silver plated photo frame. I understand that unless you hear from me, I will receive 6 superb new titles every month for just £2.10* each postage and packing free. I am under no obligation to purchase any books and I may cancel or suspend my subscription at any time, but the free books and gifts will be mine to keep in any case. (I am over 18 years of age)

N61E

Ms/Mrs/Miss/Mr _____

Address _____

_____

_____ Postcode _____

mps MAILING PREFERENCE SERVICE

MILLS & BOON®

Next Month's Romances

Each month you can choose from a wide variety of romance with Mills & Boon. Below are the new titles to look out for next month in our two new series Presents and Enchanted.

Presents™

BEST MAN TO WED?	Penny Jordan
THE MIRROR BRIDE	Robyn Donald
MARRIED TO THE MAN	Ann Charlton
WEDDING FEVER	Lee Wilkinson
RECKLESS FLIRTATION	Helen Brooks
HIS COUSIN'S WIFE	Lynsey Stevens
A SUITABLE MISTRESS	Cathy Williams
CARMICHAEL'S RETURN	Lilian Peake

Enchanted™

WITH HIS RING	Jessica Steele
THE MARRIAGE RISK	Debbie Macomber
RUNAWAY WEDDING	Ruth Jean Dale
AVOIDING MR RIGHT	Sophie Weston
THE ONLY MAN FOR MAGGIE	Leigh Michaels
FAMILY MAN	Rosemary Carter
CLANTON'S WOMAN	Patricia Knoll
THE BEST MAN FOR LINZI	Miriam Macgregor